Survival Rates

Winner of the

Flannery O'Connor Award

for Short Fiction

Survival Rates

STORIES BY MARY CLYDE

The University of Georgia Press

Athens and London

Published by the University of Georgia Press
Athens, Georgia 30602

Designed by Erin Kirk New
Set in 10 on 14 Berkeley Old Style Medium
Printed and bound by Maple-Vail Book Group, Inc.
The paper in this book meets the guidelines for
permanence and durability of the Committee on
Production Guidelines for Book Longevity of the
Council on Library Resources.

Printed in the United States of America

03 02 01 00 99 C 5 4 3 2

Library of Congress Cataloging in Publication Data

Clyde, Mary.
Survival rates : stories / by Mary Clyde.
p. cm.
"Winner of the Flannery O'Connor Award for
short fiction"—Prelim.
p.
Contents: Howard Johnson's house—Krista had
a treble clef rose—A good paved road—Victor's funeral
urn—Pruitt love—Survival rates—Farming butterflies—
Heartbreak house—Jumping.
ISBN 0-8203-2049-8 (alk. paper)
PS3553.L93S8 1999
813'.54—dc21 98-19074

British Library Cataloging in Publication Data available

For Michael

Acknowledgments

Some of these stories first appeared in magazines: "Farming Butterflies" in *Writers' Forum,* "Krista Had a Treble Clef Rose" in *Boulevard*, "A Good Paved Road" in *Quarterly West,* and "Jumping" in *Georgia Review.*

The author also gratefully acknowledges the MFA Writing Program at Vermont College, especially Darrell Spencer, Sydney Lea, François Camoin, and Sena Jeter Naslund for support and wise guidance.

Contents

Survival Rates

Howard Johnson's House

At a time when *environment* simply meant *surroundings*, Howard Johnson, the hotelier, used dynamite to gouge a foothold for his mansion overlooking Paradise Valley. He built a carport to accommodate six automobiles, including his favorite, a white Lincoln Continental, its windows dark and mirrored. He enclosed the cement balcony with wedding cake railings that occasionally saved inebriated guests from toppling into the pale, hardscrabble desert below. When he sold the house, the neighbors lower on Phoenix Mountain were optimistic. At last, they said, someone will get rid of the orange roof.

///

The mansion is now calm and almost dark behind its swimming pool moat. The beam from a security light is fractured in the ripples of the spa. Here is the peace of wealth. Cecil sits on the raw silk comforter of the king-size bed, shaking his knotted gold cuff links like dice, an unconscious wish for better luck.

Beth says, "But what's she dying of?" Beth is nestled in the bed's assortment of pillows: brocade, tapestry, needlepoint—her decorator's studied mismatch.

Cecil says, "She won't tell me."

Beth's black-framed reading glasses are new since their wedding two years ago. Her elbow rests on a velvet pillow menacingly embroidered NOT TONIGHT.

Cecil walks into his closet. A stack of unread *JAMA*s leans against the black plaid golf bag. He crumples his shirt into the pile.

"You can phone Dick in the morning," Beth calls.

"She has a new doctor. She said it was time to be independent. She wants to take charge." His mother had made it sound like getting hired for a first job. That's what amazed him more than anything: she seemed less frightened than proud, invigorated. He pictures Edna's face as she told him, her smile crisp as hotel linen. "Dear," she'd said, "I'm very ill. It's *t-e-r-m-i-n-a-l*." And he'd thought, actually prayed, *Please, please let me be good. This time. Let me rise to this and do the right thing*. But he also thought—and he was ashamed to admit it—*why did she have to spell it?*

Beth enters his closet, straightens a tie on the rotating rack—a tie that reveals Cecil's first wife's strange taste. It has squiggles like anxious sperm. Beth says, "What are you going to do?"

What he must do—urgently, *must* do—is be the best son he can be. He must find a way not to be irritated by his mother. This is a test, from God or Edna, a test he will pass.

"What do you think I should do?" he says.

"I think you should find out: (a) what she's dying of and (b) what she wants you to do for her." Beth often alphabetizes answers.

But it makes sense, and it *sounds* simple. His spirits lift until he thinks of Edna, standing in the foyer of Symphony Hall after spelling out her doom. She was wearing a bright lime jacket with dark braid on the lapels and with pearl buttons. Apricot and lime green, she's explained, are secret code colors of wealth and good taste.

Sipping Dr. Pepper: "It's a fine production," she said of a tired and sound-distorted *Grease*. "Don't you think Zuko is authentic?" She put her hand, suddenly, on his arm. "I had to change doctors. Dick misses things."

Cecil sensed her energy then, focused and precise, even as she was talking about her death. "What has Dick missed?"

"Phh," she said, an exhale ruffling her lips, indicating Dick's omissions were too numerous and odious to mention. "I don't want you and Ted to worry about me." By which he knew that's precisely what she wanted—as well as attention; she was dying for it.

"Homosexuals," she said, way too loudly, "isn't it interesting how they like theater? Why do you think that is?" Edna's specialty: asking questions that deserve no answer. Also, affectations of broad-mindedness.

Now Beth dumps the pillows off the bed like unwelcome pets. A little yoga and a lot of money seem to have made her serene. She says, "She's probably just trying to be brave."

Edna brave? Not likely. Cecil thinks of her terror at his father's funeral, the gulping sobs like drowning and then a last-minute refusal to let the casket be lowered. "I just can't do that to him," she'd said, the heels of her small black pumps sinking into the soggy earth and the vein in her temple throbbing. And Ted with his always too-long hair said, unhelpfully, "Mom, you don't have to," which was after all—Cecil remembers—the tack that finally worked.

He struggles to consider her as simply another human being. Distance, he feels, would help him do better. But just as he can't imagine Edna's pride and joy, the silver and crystal candlesticks, ever belonging to anyone else, she is only his and Ted's. Her past choices so old they seem to never have been decisions at all, just circumstances that have always existed. She has always said *taupe* when *brown* would have done, and *burgundy* instead of *red*. She has always salted lettuce and sipped Dr. Pepper. But *death*. That's making Edna something else. Because she is dying, suddenly she has life. Still exasperating, still impossible, but exposing him, making him accountable.

Beth touches his face. Her cool fingers slide to his jaw. She says, "I'm taking a bath."

He walks to the window and looks past the city lights to the dark, prehistoric hulk of Camelback Mountain. There is a light where the camel's ears might be. Campfire, hikers. The Search and Rescue team bills them when they have to risk their own lives getting them down.

My mother is dying, he thinks, and he's chagrined to realize all he feels is extremely tired.

/ / /

Beth has begged him to have it replaced. "It's a roof, Cecil," she's said. "And it's orange." But when he bought the house he was recently divorced and undone by failure as well as hope. He'd walked through the empty rooms and thought of the man who built them. He read about Johnson, how critics announced that he was not like his father, the restaurant's founder. They called the younger Johnson an accountant, but said his father was clever, an entrepreneur with vision. The business began to fail when the son stuck with the stodgy menu; everyone—Denny's, Marriott, Big Boy—diversified. Restaurants specialized. They became ethnic, regional, or themed. They offered a variety of single menu items. How could Howard Johnson's compete with Baskin-Robbins' reckless imagination?

But Cecil was vicariously proud of his Johnson's accomplishments. The restaurants had a plain, homey comfort. Nice, clean restrooms. The orange roofs signaled that: something happy and decent. He fancies families dining with fresh-scrubbed faces, the boys wearing boxy jeans with cuffs rolled wide—the kind he'd wanted to wear, but Edna called too ugly.

Cecil finds he's fond of Howard Johnson. He feels he understands him, often calls him Howard. He is unsettled, however, when he tries to remember eating at a Howard Johnson's, because he can't recall a single time.

/ / /

Pajamas soaked from urine or sweat—he's too scared to know which—five years old and he tells Edna his nightmare. "Dreams come true in the opposite," she said. "So it just means that someday you will swim fast and eat up a big shark." Then she smiled as if something had been settled and left him sitting in the dark.

/ / /

It's from a dog bite. The nose has been degloved; the cartilage destroyed. The patient, only nine, has blond too-thick hair. Her mother is agitated, anxious to declare her confidence in Cecil and to lament the tragedy that has befallen her only child.

"She's a beautiful girl," she says, looking at her daughter with conviction—truckfuls of dizzying mother's hope.

His examining room is too ordinary for the excesses of this drama. The nubby carpet and high-backed vinyl chairs, the barren cleanliness seem designed to discourage or deny suffering. Cecil takes paper from the wall desk. He nudges the rolling stool back toward the girl and begins to sketch the reconstruction. "It'll take at least two surgeries," he says.

When he glances at the girl, she's looking at him carefully, as if she's going to draw him. Cecil tells about taking cartilage from a rib, rotating a flap of skin from the forehead to cover it. The mother says they understand.

The surgery is scheduled. The yellow insurance sheet torn off, hands shaken, pre-op is left to be discussed with the nurse. Halfway out the door Cecil turns back: "If you happen to have a photograph. Or can get me one. It can help."

Eagerly, the mother opens her purse, slips the picture into Cecil's hand.

Verdant foliage seems to choke the other surroundings. To Cecil so much green looks desperate, false as hair dyed black. His patient is squatting and appears to have been examining something just out of the camera's view. Now she looks up through sun-bleached bangs, not with irritation, but with the lingering pleasure of her discovery and also expectantly, as if what life offers is dependably good. Her face is shadowed by the suffocating green, but her nose is in the clearest light.

It may be the ugliest child's nose Cecil has ever seen. In French cuisine, it would be scrambled eggs doused with ketchup. In classic automobiles, it would be a Gremlin disfigured with body putty. She has a nose like a golf club—a one wood. Too thin, then too round, and full at the tip.

///

At the party, Cecil is showing the aerial photograph Howard Johnson had someone take of the house. The bedroom roofs fan out like a fluted fruit bowl.

"How would you ever think of an orange roof?" says Andrea, an anesthesiologist's wife, whose too-small nose is Mark Myer's work.

Cecil's giving a tour. He's shown the saltwater fish aquarium, with its pulsing sea anemone and fluorescent pink starfish. Then the kitchen where the fireplace is large enough to roast a boar, according to a *Southwest Home* article. In the living room Cecil motions toward the view, the cactus-studded mountains with their sudden bizarre rock formations. He feels daring living here, where the landscape doesn't want to be inhabited and seems to wait patiently for him—for all of them—to go.

"Incredible," someone sighs.

The sandy-haired anesthesiologist says, "Do you suppose the McDonald brothers' houses had golden arches?"

Cecil says, "Howard Johnson's took off when Johnson senior added butterfat to his ice cream flavors: vanilla, chocolate, and strawberry." Cecil knows this brings all conversation to a bored standstill, and Beth has asked him not to do it. But the story is so straightforward and gratifying.

He can hear Beth laugh, a group away. "Thongs, I say, should be worn only on feet."

He turns and in doing so bumps into a young woman who he sees has been waiting to catch his attention. She has the grim look of an overachiever. Her handshake is determined. She tells him her name, a man's name, which he instantly forgets. She explains that she's in a plastic surgery residency at the Mayo Clinic. "What I'd like to know," she says, "what I can't resist this opportunity to ask you—is what you consider the key to a successful rhinoplasty." Her eagerness makes him feel as if he's been asked the secret of life.

Cecil considers giving her the conventional answers: that a nose needs to match its owner; that the dorsum must have a gentle break. But maybe because it's a party, or perhaps because she's so young and overzealous, instead he laughs: "It's so much fun."

The woman—isn't she a girl really?—cocks her head. Perplexed.

He says, "It's like being able to change ugly ducklings into swans. When you consider what you can do with just a tuck at the nostril or by resloping the bridge!" He pauses to savor the pleasure of it, a thrill he's certain only the best in his field know.

But the young doctor frowns. "A fairy godfather thing?" This is not what she'd hoped for.

"Yes!" Cecil ignores her disappointment. "I can grant the wish for a perfect nose."

He's grabbed by the lawyer who set up his corporation. She asks if he thinks her forehead is falling. Beth walks toward him, graceful and careful, like a headdressed showgirl. "You preaching noses?"

"I was asked."

She rolls her eyes, but smiles. "Ted called."

"Did he leave a number?"

She pauses. Silver bracelets jingle as she waves to someone across the room. "Says he's on the road. He'll call you."

Ted being on the road might mean a new job, a lost job, a move, a marriage. Ted thrives on big change and long odds. He's content in the way only dreamers are. Ted will put his arm around Cecil's shoulders and call him Sport, an affectation Cecil means to find irritating but always enjoys instead.

"Does he know anything about Mother? Has she told him

what the disease is?" He thinks of Edna, whose footing, he decides, seems unsure. A consequence of his not knowing what she's dying of is that she seems to have symptoms of everything.

"Ted doesn't know any more than you do." Beth pulls off a spangled earring, repinches it onto her ear. She nods toward their company. "How soon do you suppose they'll go home?"

/ / /

Edna says *fine* is for wine, art, and china, but not for the weather. She says *smuck* for *schmuck*. And before she stopped suddenly: *e-lec-twis-ity*. Cecil can't imagine who corrected her.

/ / /

Horrified, the mother says, "It looks like a tongue growing out of her forehead. Is there anything you can do in the meantime?"

Cecil says, "We have to leave it like that until it establishes its own blood supply. Then we'll amputate it by the bridge, and we can start to sculpt it." He clicks on his penlight, scoots his stool toward his patient. He's been looking at the mother, searching for clues as to where the girl's original nose came from, but the mother's nose is ordinary, with a slight rise at the bridge.

The girl continues to watch him thoughtfully, even sympathetically, as if she knows his secrets. More likely, he thinks, she has her own. He examines the tissue with his light and is satisfied it is healthy. He wonders why the girl didn't complain about the other children's taunts. Surely, all of her life she's been teased about her nose. Was she saving her mother or herself?

"Mrs. Martin," he says, clicking off the light, "this is going to take some patience. And her nose won't be the same as it was before."

The mother sputters. Her voice husky with despair, she says,

"You're supposed to be the best. My husband says they call you The Nose."

The girl brightens. "That's what they always call *me*."

/ / /

Beth enjoys nice things. Cecil thinks this with pride and a twinge of miserly alarm as he notices new mosaic vases flanking the stone fireplace. "Do you like them?" she says, coming up behind him. "They were quite a find."

Since she moved in, she and her decorator have undertaken a room-by-room redo. Gone are the bright red leather sofas he'd had made. "Howard Johnson had some like them," he'd said weakly in their defense. "Cowboy boots aren't quite the look we want," the decorator said with such disdain Cecil was intimidated and knew she must be good.

He's also a little scared of Beth, his former travel agent, who one day included with his ticket to the Canary Islands a printed card saying she had changed her name from Marilyn to Beth. Getting to know her better, he'd hoped for an explanation that has never come. He doesn't know why people would change their names, or even what it means to want to. But he's sure her ability to slough off a name proves she's capable in ways he can't imagine being. Her decisiveness and self-assurance are the traits he'd say attracted him to her. Her answers. Sometimes he fears the only thing he knows for certain is how to correct a nose.

"Reproductions?" Cecil says, hopefully, of the vases.

"Reproductions of what?"

"Something more expensive?"

Beth's smile is elusive. "The colors blend so nicely with the view, don't you think? Desert colors. Cold, pale browns, harsh greens."

Cecil thinks it sounds a little ominous. Rattlesnakes, he imagines, scorpions. He watches Beth look into the desert. He's close enough to see how the red cast of her hair makes her eyes a sharper blue, but he can't tell what she's thinking. His first wife was a librarian. You know where you stand with a librarian, he thinks.

"Should we go out for dinner?" she says, arranging bare swirly branches in the vases.

"How about takeout?" He's exhausted.

Beth frowns. "Long day?"

He's had a letter from his patient's mother, a rant about good faith, an admonition that he will not "play God" with her child's nose. She says she sees what he's trying to do.

"Beth, what would you do—" he starts to ask about his patient, but he finds he knows her answer will be to send the girl to someone else. She will tell him that with a mother like that, helping the girl is too risky. It could have serious consequences. It's true, of course. But suddenly he can't stand to hear it, can't stand to think what this says about Beth—that a certain dispassionate objectivity would allow her to abandon the girl; that her decisions can be based on mere expediency. He switches topics: "Mom's obsessed with getting a will drafted."

Beth's look says, So what's the matter with that?

"Beth, she doesn't have enough to bother with."

"But it will give her a sense of closure. It will make her feel as if she does."

His mother is doing it for attention, he thinks. He feels sullen but also ashamed of the stubborn stinginess that won't allow him to feign the concern she craves.

Beth says, "It's easy to make Edna feel important." She is always solicitous toward his mother. "Edna, take this chair," she says, ushering her over to it. And Edna will situate herself, in her new, fragile body, flashing Beth one of her not-long-for-this-world smiles of appreciation. His mother looks like she's lost weight, he thinks, oddly wishing for one of his own before-surgery pictures for comparison. She's paler, too, of that he's sure.

"You need to be patient with her," Beth says. "I'll get the take-out menus."

He goes to the fireplace and sees the new vases are made of shards of old china. On one fragment there is gold lettering that spells *Tuesday;* another has a beige fleur-de-lis. One piece has the gray-green stripe of a Depression-era cafeteria mug. Why, it could be from a Howard Johnson's, he thinks. Pleased, he puts his mother out of his mind.

/ / /

Cecil and Edna sit in her living room. With its careful arrangement of long-waisted ballerina figurines on a distress-finished table, it is Edna's idea of someone else's idea of appealing. A room like Edna, begging to be thought well of.

She has given him a cup of tea in her pink art deco china. With a dull panic, he notices red pinpoints on her hand, which he thinks he remembers are a sign of a blood disease. He'd like to blurt, What is your illness? But he sees that her determination to keep it secret is a perversity she treasures.

"I hope Beth will enjoy this set," Edna says, lifting a cup toward him. She has been sorting her belongings into teetering piles. Cecil realizes that if she weren't Edna he would see how sad this is; he would feel pity. Oddly, he could do better then, be more patient and tolerant. But pitying his mother—even if he could—would open some immense family floodgate that they would all slip through, helpless as trout. Something fragile is maintained in his reserve.

"I've found some things of your father's. One is a wallet you made for him at summer camp. He never used it," she adds flatly.

"Ted made it," Cecil says, handing it back, though he has no idea where it came from.

When he was ten Edna taught him to polka, after first insisting he wash his face and hands and comb his hair. Now, as he remembers it, it is not just the living room furniture that whirls by, but his growing up, his life. The card games she taught them with complicated, contradictory rules. "Salamander," she'd yell suddenly, her bangs permed like poodle fluff, her cards flying like bats. ("Turn your head, too," she said, as they polkaed. "Next time we'll roll up the rug.") She cut their hair in the bathtub, then powdered them with Lily of the Valley. Ted begged to be spared the powder. She replied, "Silliest of boys." (An animal's name—a billy goat? a bear?—in the polka's title helped make it seem more fun.) Then the thread was taut before she bit it. "I hope you like it, dear," she said to his first wife about a homemade skirt Andrea wore to the library even after she got her Neiman's charge. The dance ending, Cecil rug-burned an elbow in a dizzy fall. "Stop that racket," his father yelled from the basement. Cecil supposes that was when he discovered that accordions were embarrassing and also a little sad.

". . . those cookies I used to make at Christmas. Do you remember the year you ate them all? And Ted told on you?" Her laugh represents a past she wants them to have shared. She says Ted's coming next week. She says she killed a black widow in the bathroom. But her chatter only communicates one thing to him: her last-chance hope for his love.

He wonders when he got old enough that the failure of this relationship became his failure and no longer hers. How old was he when she called him *Cecil-Weasel?* And didn't he love her then? He searches for a day, a moment—some concrete time—where her foolishness and her vanity, where the irritations of who she is overwhelmed his dutiful affection. When did his soul become so destitute? A son who does not love his mother.

Maybe it happened when he started medical school and she began to call him *doctor*—not because her addressing him as doctor was pretentious and slightly mortifying, but because suddenly he was important. She adored him. Did he reject her because he guessed her love was based more on his status as a future physician than on who he really was? *My son, the doctor.* Or perhaps his failure came later, during his residency. Did he despise Edna because the glamorous speciality so delighted her? *My son, the plastic surgeon!* Did it happen when he understood that he didn't intend to dedicate his life to transforming the ropy patches of burn victims? Did he fear he'd inherited her dubious ideals? Did Cecil hate Edna because her love was, after all, based precisely on who he really was?

Why wasn't she the right kind of mother? But also, why wasn't he the right kind of son?

"Beth sent this over," he says, remembering the fruit basket she had shoved into his hands. "Take credit for it," she had said.

"How thoughtful she is," Edna says. She picks up an apple, rubs the skin to make it squeak. "An apple for your thoughts," she says.

His frustration is so strong he thinks it leaves a taste—a taste dusty and sharp, the bad flavor of a shriveled walnut.

"Penny," he gasps. "Mom, it's a penny for your thoughts." He begs it.

/ / /

As they leave the examining room, the mother says, "You'll pay for this."

In the absurd objective thinking of such times, Cecil decides, *melodramatic*.

Before she's yanked out, the daughter shyly waves.

He sits on his examining table, clicking his penlight off and on. He shines it on the wastebasket lid, flashes it on the sinuses of the cross-section diagram, says out loud, "What have I done?" He doesn't even know her, this other Nose. He thinks it's the photograph that got him here, the hopeful way she looked up. She deserved something. He's glad about her wave.

He puts the light in his pocket, pats his hospital identification badge. He'd like to think of himself as a man of principle. He has done, and will stand by doing, the right thing. But this feels quaint and ineffectual, a Boy Scout reciting his oath. If good is triumphing somewhere, he guesses it has more to do with luck than choice or God.

The sad irony is that the nose turned out better than he had hoped—the skin blending surprisingly well, the new shape transforming the girl's appearance like a fable. The nose is a miracle. "It was the best I could do," he says, rehearsing his testimony. "The nose was like a golf club," he says, knowing he won't and can't say it in court.

"It was obvious." He eases himself off the table and shoves the stool back under the desk.

/ / /

Edna wept when he left his first wife. She said, "I wish I knew where this might lead."

Cecil said, "I knew where it *was* leading, Mother. I knew it was something I just couldn't fix."

/ / /

Beth's voice is a shrill soprano that twists in Cecil's chest. They are singing "Happy Birthday" to Edna on his balcony. Beth's smile is cheerful as the expensive birthday cake with puffy frosting carrots fake as Bugs Bunny's.

"Should I blow them out?" Edna says before she does. She wears a pendant with an abstract shape like an internal organ. Liver, he thinks. No, pituitary gland. She pats it whenever something excites her.

Cecil admits it: today his mother appears ill. She no longer fusses as before with the gauze pad taped to the crook of her arm. Dying seems to have lost its novelty. She has a peaked look of fear.

She says Ted's arrival has been postponed for just a week or two, studiously overlooking how Ted has been unavoidably delayed four times already. Cecil watches as she turns toward the desert. He thinks the mountains seem close today, particularly inhospitable in the noon light. The olive green of the saguaros reminds him of a tank's armor, and there's a glare that makes him feel thirsty.

Edna nods toward the Praying Monk, a huge sandstone formation on Camelback Mountain. Its devout posture is marred today by rock climbers on belay. "What are they doing up there?"

"Climbing," Cecil says.

"Why would they do that?" She laughs, but is, in fact, expecting some answer.

"I'm being sued for negligence," Cecil says.

Beth looks up from her cake. "Negligence?"

"Gross negligence is the exact terminology. I expect to lose."

Beth and Edna seem stunned. He sees he's disillusioned them in ways they'd never imagined.

Beth's voice is gentle. "Surely there's something you can do?"

"I can operate again, give the child an ugly nose, but I'm not going to."

Beth says, "Let's think about this."

Edna whispers, "But what about me?"

"Edna!" Beth flashes her a look of displeasure so sharp that Cecil flinches. He sees a pretense slip, Beth's animosity for Edna exposed. He understands suddenly how he's depended on Beth, counted on her doing the right thing with his mother. She has been his conscience, but this conscience, he sees, is based on what is easy, not on what is honest or even right. A conscience without feeling. Beth smooths the hair at her temples, a gesture he knows is calculated to restore her composure. But watching it, he imagines her adjusting a mask, adroitly blending the edges into her hair.

Cecil looks at his shoes. They are falsely rugged, like his expensive all-terrain vehicle that has never been off asphalt. Like Beth, whose real name is Marilyn. He looks at his mother. Her face is pale. Her mouth quivers. He is all she has.

"What is your illness, Mother?" he says.

Her hand flutters to her necklace. "Leukemia," she says, a surrender reverent as a prayer.

A breeze ruffles the fringe of the table's umbrella and tosses Edna's crumpled napkin. He waits to feel love for his mother. Now that he knows what she's dying of. Now that he knows it is real. He thinks it could come like a spirit, floating from some heavenly height. A form with iridescence, like the rainbow shiver of oil on water. Maybe the Holy Spirit. But there is nothing.

"Oh, God," he says. He thinks of the rattlesnakes on the

mountain, their bodies fat as a man's arm. They suddenly seem real and close. "Ted won't come, Mom," he says, this final, necessary cruelty. "He'll leave this to me. I'm sorry."

Beth says, "Cecil, stop."

He expects Edna to weep, but she does not. She holds her head in a way that seems brave. In her courage—or the sad, limp imitation of it—he sees she deserves some kind of love, and he wishes love were about what is deserved or earned. He wishes love could be awarded.

/ / /

Three months later Cecil is in a booth meant for a family, where their sliding in would look comical, ending with the mother getting the last seat by a high-chaired baby. But Cecil is here alone. The menu is in a greasy plastic cover. The waitress looks so much like a waitress that Cecil believes serving tables was her only possible choice. She is a cliché of swollen ankles and bobby-pinned hair. She calls him *hon,* an unconsidered intimacy from overwork and another era, but it touches him.

As he expected, the entrees are out of style: chicken cacciatore with "savory herb blends from Italy" and spiced baked ham with pineapple rings. No little red heart-smart labels in sight. An industry analyst in *Hotel Management* said that Howard Johnson could have saved the business if he'd eaten at his own restaurants instead of lunching at 21.

"Spaghetti," Cecil says, pointing, as if the menu is in a language he doesn't trust himself to pronounce.

She nods with grave approval. "Coffee with that, hon?"

The place is almost empty, just off I-10 where drivers can spot the orange roof.

Cecil says, "Howard Johnson started out with three ice cream flavors in a store by a commuter rail station."

She nods, pleasant but uninterested. Even her nose is a waitress's, with a look of habitual romantic disappointment.

"I live in a house Howard Johnson built," Cecil says.

"No kidding?" This time she's not just being polite. "Where?"

"It has an orange roof."

She squints to see if he's teasing, but then is somehow convinced. "No way!"

"Each bedroom has its own outside entrance and a bathroom with a phone."

"Like a hotel!" she exclaims, as if it's the punch line.

"Howard had a lot of guests. Business, of course, but he was really a nice guy. Honest and generous. People liked him."

"You knew him?" She's impressed.

"My mother died last Wednesday," he says, before he can stop himself or even think to try.

"I'm so sorry." She folds her arms for a respectful moment. "I'll bring your coffee. Losing a mother. That's hard."

After she's left he looks out the window. Near the entrance, orange lantana sprouts hopefully from the hard-packed bare ground. A couple of bedraggled palms shade the door. A car angles into the handicapped parking space.

The waitress, whose name tag reads EDDIE, returns with his coffee. "On the house, hon," she announces proudly, but also sympathetically.

"No, no." He is undeserving. "I couldn't possibly. It's too much," he says, because suddenly it really is.

Krista Had a Treble Clef Rose

Anne and Nicole at Lunch

Perched on bar stools at Johnny Rockets Diner, Anne tugs at the lettuce ruffle of her sandwich; Nicole smears a puddle of ketchup with a French fry.

"We're freaks," Anne announces. She says it mildly. Though she believes it, she's said it before.

"We are." Nicole's slow nod accelerates in agreement.

Poster teenagers, they call themselves, though they're not. Still, they are aware it's only the survivors who get to represent their disease.

A girl in cutoff jeans and combat boots pauses in front of the frantic shapes of a mall theater's movie posters.

"Cute hair," Anne whispers. She straightens the turquoise shopping bag resting by her sandaled feet. Inside is a clam comb of imitation tortoiseshell and wands like chopsticks to twist up her hair.

Nicole says, "The anesthesia made my hair fall out. I've got three hairs left. I'm playing up my eyes." She bats them as proof. Then: "Dr. Stafford is the cutest of the junior doctors. Don't you think? He told me I reminded him of his sister-in-law."

"Except when he pulled my wound drain, he didn't warn me."

Nicole sighs. "The Jackson Pratt drain."

They wince and smile, knowing smiles of well-tended teeth.

Nine months ago, they were Garden Grove Honor Cotillion Debutantes. Anne had giggled when she told her mother about her nomination because wasn't she just exactly not the type? But wasn't it a kick to be one?

Anne now says, "My dad wants to buy me clothes. Suddenly he can't buy me enough clothes."

Nicole says, "My mom will say, 'Would you like something to eat, sweetie?' Then doesn't even blink. Brings it like some genie and stands there watching me eat."

"They feel guilty."

"It's no one's fault."

"We're not going to die, not now."

"Saved by stomas."

"Ileostomies," Anne says, a word that suddenly sounds like a flying dinosaur.

Anne's Boyfriend

Anne's boyfriend Jeff left for college while she was still in the hospital. Before he left he visited her often and brought roses in a vase. Like a wedding anniversary or an apology for forgetting one. Florist flowers, but all different colors, which showed he had no taste. Part of why she liked him, that he didn't pretend he did.

When an alarm sounded, he ran to get the nurse. "It's just a pump," Anne called, but he was already in the hall. He played ice hockey; he was fast even without his skates.

They went for walks in the halls. Jeff pushed the IV pole and kept a wary eye on the pumps. He was prone to giving himself titles: Amazing Microwave Chef, Consumer Math Repeat Kid. "Supreme IV Pole Navigator," he now said. His smile looked like his old smile, goofy and a little shy. It made her miss him and understand how that part of him was already gone.

Once they rode the elevator to the cafeteria. The cashier spotted some label on Anne's equipment and radioed for help. It came in the fast-moving form of an efficient Asian nurse.

"Must not leave floor," she scolded, wresting the IV pole from the startled Jeff. "Never, never. You N.P.O."

Nothing by mouth. It sounded contagious, deadly.

Anne said, "You think I'd eat something?"

"Been done," the nurse said, commandeering the IV pole.

Jeff looked as if he might cry.

What to Wear in the Hospital

As her condition worsened, Anne abandoned her appearance. She quit plucking her eyebrows, didn't bother with her contact lenses, sent home her makeup and earrings and her nightshirts with a prostrate Snoopy and Jesus Christ as a superstar.

It took concentration to stay alive. She wore hospital gowns because of their utility and as an admission of how sick she was and because she now belonged. Soldiers wear fatigues. She rolled up her sleeves, lost the knack of good looks, forgot the need.

When she came home from the hospital, just shaving her legs exhausted her.

Anne's Father and Mother

Afterward, she heard her father whisper in the hall, "Do you think she understands?"

Her mother said, "Do you?" It sounded fierce.

The Psychiatrist Visits

The psychiatrist told her about his brother who had been hospitalized with the same thing when he was a young boy. "They took him off food, too." The psychiatrist untangled her IV tubes, expertly. He said he didn't want to see the photographs of her ulcerated colon, but the way he said it was kind, and made Anne hope the pictures weren't as important as the doctors made them out to be. "My brother watched TV all day. It was when McDonald's was just introducing Chicken McNuggets. All he talked about was how when he got out he'd get some. It helped him get through it, gave him something to look forward to."

(Talk to him, her mother had pleaded before he came in. "Annie, just try. He can help you.")

Tubes brought things into Anne's body, other tubes took things out. It seemed like math, a hospital story problem: "If a teenager is not responding to medication and has two tubes for feeding and one tube for blood, and if the tube in her nose. . . ."

"Anne," the psychiatrist said, "visualize a healthy colon."

Anne and Nicole Go Shopping at J. Crew

Anne buys a high-waisted dress of fluttery fabric with the colors and spots of overripe bananas.

"Is it too short?" she says.

Nicole shakes her head. "You've got nice legs."

"Look how my calves go in. Right there. Look how deformed."

Nicole holds out her freckled arms. "You think that's bad? Look at my fat arms." Anne has seen Nicole's mother; she has seen these arms before. "And my knees are kind of baggy." Nicole pinches her knees where Anne now notices they sag, something like a zoo elephant's.

What to Expect Before Surgery

The enterostomal therapy nurse will visit your hospital room to mark the ileostomy site. The placement is based on several factors: skin creases, scars, navel, waistline, hip bone, how you sit and where you wear the waist of your clothes. Proper location makes ileostomy care easier after the surgery.

Food Dreams

Frequently: mashed potatoes—the gastro-intestinal patient's last food friend.

Occasionally: Chocolate Cornflake Crunchies. Anne's mother hadn't made them since kindergarten. Anne thought she'd forgotten them, didn't remember even liking them; now she had Chocolate Cornflake Crunchy fantasies. A steep yearning, sweet as homesickness.

Recurring nightmare: Popcorn—salted, buttered, white-cheddar-cheesed, carameled, balled, pink-candied. She'd been told she could never eat popcorn again, which scared her and proved her vulnerability as nothing else quite had. Because who could be undone by popcorn?

Friends

Krista had a treble clef rose, a tattoo three inches long on her thigh, because she was going to major in music.

Jen had blown out her knee cheerleading, but she refused to have it operated on until after basketball season. As a concession to her parents she wore a brace for tumbling.

Richard said he'd been born with an extra finger. Its ghost helped him catch. It gave him ESP.

Anne's Father at the Hospital

Sometimes her father seemed as difficult as the illness. He washed her undriven car and replaced the burnt-out taillight. He bought her a Rolling Stones CD. Mick Jagger looked desperate.

He brought Misty, their golden retriever, who stood beneath Anne's hospital window, dismayed by the circumstances. She sniffed the air. When a doctor knelt to pet her, she gratefully wagged her tail.

When Anne's pain was intense, she thought no one else could have ever experienced anything like it. She learned what morphine demanded in exchange for its not-quite-heroic rescue. She worried about becoming addicted.

Her father's experience with pain medication included the nitrous oxide from the dentist and Tylenol with codeine from the time he broke his leg skiing. "I heard it snap," he said, still in fond disbelief.

"Annie, what can I do for you?" he said.

Out of kindness, she or her mother came up with errands: lotion from home? a blanket from the warmer? He forgot them. Instead, he wired her hospital room for stereo sound from the VCR and replumbed the bathroom shower.

"This way," he yelled over the clank of his tools, "when you're ready for a shower, you can direct the spray."

Hospital Routine

The hospital gave medication, recorded vital signs, changed linens, and offered sponge baths on a rigid schedule.

Unscheduled but with frequency, Anne bled, cursed, wept, vomited, and prayed. Whatever she did the staff called her brave, and she understood how saying it helped them.

The Boyfriend Leaves for College

Anne wore white surgical support stockings and two hospital gowns. Jeff wore a baseball cap. The logo was *No Fear.* They walked by the surgery waiting room, where the occupants regarded their progress with ill-concealed anxiety or encouragement.

Back in Anne's room, Jeff sat in the chair one of her parents slept in at night. He stroked the IV pole and told Anne about work at the furniture rental store. How his dad kept asking what kind of people have to rent furniture. Anne realized a boyfriend was an exhausting luxury like reading or crossword puzzles.

Jeff didn't talk about how he was going away to school, which proved to her how badly he wanted to talk about it, how eager he was to go. He didn't talk about Anne either, but she knew he watched her carefully to see what she expected or wanted from him and if she were in any way still the same.

She thought, *We are in love* and also, *This relationship is probably doomed.*

Anne and Nicole Shop at the Sports Watch Counter

Nicole says her goal is to kiss a guy of every race. Every religion, too. "But with a system," she says, "like starting with boys from extreme far-right religions and going to extreme left. Or from short guys to tall ones. Something to make it challenging."

The watch Anne is looking at doesn't have numbers, but has weird geometric shapes instead.

"Or older men to younger," Nicole says, taking the watch from Anne. "That way I'd be shocking when I was young fooling around with old men and again when I was old, kissing young guys."

Anne says, "Do all religions allow kissing?"

"Who could be against kissing?"

"I don't know. Amish? Do they?" Anne says.

"Yuck, who'd want to kiss some Amish guy?"

Anne takes the watch back. "Do you think after I got used to this watch I'd be able to tell time on it?"

"I mean he'd never forget me, an Amish boy. He'd be so grateful."

Mother of pearl makes one watch face appear chaste. Another is no bigger than an aspirin.

Anne says, "I'd like something plain, but gorgeous."

Nicole's Mother

Nicole's mother banned popcorn from the house, as if it were responsible. When the popcorn ads were flashed before movies, Nicole said her mother clucked her tongue and said, "Honestly!" the same as she did for cigarette or beer ads. Popcorn became a vice.

Nicole's parents were divorced. Her father moved to New Mexico and kept urging her to join him, telling her how the fresh mountain air and exercise could help her. Once her mother yanked the phone out of Nicole's hand. "Rodney," she screamed, "she doesn't have tuberculosis!"

Anne's Mother

Anne found even if she didn't respond to her mother, her mother continued to talk to her. She jabbered cheerfully. Anne hadn't thought her mother was a jabberer. Sometimes she didn't bother to listen while her mother changed her hospital gowns or shampooed her hair. She looked away when her mother bathed her, her earlier modesty forgotten. Once, she thought, this must have been how she spoke to me when I was a baby before I learned to talk.

Then one day Anne heard her: "Anne," she said, "where are you when you don't answer us? Where is it you go?"

Anne looked at her mother then, saw how bruised her eyes looked; how she'd lost weight. She is suffering, Anne thought, and it frightened her.

"Sometimes I just don't feel like talking," Anne said, but she thought, I'm holding my breath; balancing on life's thin edge.

Friends

Coach hung Richard's jersey from where the rafters would be if the high school gymnasium had them. He said the team would finish the season playing in his memory. In all his years of coaching he'd never seen anything like what Richard could do to an opposition's defensive line. Coach hugged his clipboard to his chest and swore it: Richard could just plain read their freaking minds.

Nicole

Nicole threatened her brother when he wouldn't give her the TV remote control. She said she'd show him her bag. "You use what you've got," she explained sensibly to Anne. "It's what America is all about."

Nicole said she's never flying on an airplane, because what if the bag exploded? Nicole said *stoma* means mouth. Nicole's scar was purple. It puckered thick as masking tape.

A Letter from Anne's Boyfriend

Dear Anne,

I tested out of freshman English. Awesome! I've got a great roommate. He's from around here and knows about everything.

He signed it *love*, not *love you*. Anne guessed that it mattered, wondered what she could do.

Nicole's Mother and Aunt

Nicole's mother and her aunt stayed with her in the hospital. Nicole's aunt called Nicole's mother *sis* or *sister.* "Sister, you need some coffee." "Sis, it's high time we got the doctor in here." Anne asked Nicole if her aunt sometimes got grossed out. "No," Nicole said, "she's a Republican."

The Jackson Pratt Drain

Anne read about it. "Drains remove fluid from the surgical sites. Once the drainage decreases, they will be removed." It sounded simple enough, hardly brutal.

But cute Dr. Stafford knew better. She wondered what he *should* have said when he pulled the drain shaped like a lawn-mower starter from the surgically punctured hole in her side—a lawn-mower starter with a long, long deeply embedded cord.

But she couldn't find a warning that would not have alarmed her, a caution with the right amount of sympathy, words that would have bolstered her courage and respected the suffering that had come before and was about to be inflicted.

But: "This will sting a little"? No, not that.

Finding the Perfect Gown

Your cotillion dress must be pure white. Because of its variability in color, silk is not allowed. It must be sleeved. A cap sleeve is flattering and feminine. It must not have detracting decoration, such as feathers, sequins, beads, or pearls. A pearl necklace, however, is acceptable.

/ / /

Anne's dress was drop-waisted cotton brocade. Nicole's had a sweetheart neckline. It was taffeta. She said she thought the rustle of it sounded sexy and cheap, undermining the whole virgin-maiden thing. They wore slips, layers and layers of white netting.

Anne said, "If my period starts, I'll kill myself."

Nicole said, "If your period starts, you'll never find it."

Possible Recurrence

This fear hangs heavy as a stage curtain: like a cursed mythological figure, Anne may be forced to repeat this misery. But what will the surgeons cut out then? She must not think about it. She cannot stop thinking about it.

Hospital Visitors

Batman, with a plastic pectoral chest and a cape that swished like Nicole's cotillion dress. He gave Anne a picture of himself signed "With Bat wishes."

/ / /

The team mascot for a minor league ball team, a shaggy bull who kept banging his horns on the door frame. He gave her a blue and white pom-pom and a red baseball bat. He was led around by a uniformed batboy.

/ / /

Raggedy Anne from the Ice Capades, whose real red hair stuck out from under her red yarn hair. "Lose this place, babe," she said in a husky whisper.

/ / /

Anne's grandmother. She left a plate of peanut butter cookies, Anne's favorite, long after everyone else seemed to have forgotten Anne had ever eaten. Confused by Anne's mother's explanation of her condition, she sighed. "I don't understand what you're saying to me."

Leaving the Hospital

Going home from the hospital you get ostomy bags, one- or two-piece—like swimming suits. You get ostomy wafers, a spray-on skin barrier, an ointment to heal the skin the skin barrier misses, adhesive for the ostomy wafers, solvent for the adhesive. You get instruction from the enterostomal therapy nurse, long-suffering as a piano teacher. You get a subscription to *Ostomates*.

Nicole wore clear bags. Anne wore flesh-colored bags. She said she thought they were more feminine.

"What?" Nicole said. "You think they're more what?"

Friends

Johanna had ridden her bike late at night along the canal. Her killer folded her clothes neatly beside her. Johanna had signed Anne's yearbook, "See ya this summer!"

The Psychiatrist Visits

The psychiatrist tugged on his soaring-and-diving-seagulls tie and told Anne about a young woman in his parish who had the surgery, how glad she was to be well. "Anne, visualize your return to health. Visualize no more pain or bleeding."

The psychiatrist actually had the disease. It wasn't just his brother. He told Anne's mother in the hall, who told Anne after he'd left.

"Why didn't he just tell me himself?" Anne said.

"Maybe he thinks it would undermine his authority," her mother said.

"Because I'd know he got sick?" Anne was being what her mother called petulant. But she knew she'd slipped, like Alice, into a world with its own nonsensical rules.

"How sick?" she said. "Can he eat popcorn? Does he wear a bag?"

"Can't you call it an appliance?" Her mother turned toward the window.

Personal Ads in Ostomates

Female, 32. Diagnosed with colitis at 18. Colon cancer discovered two years ago. Had ileostomy and pull-through. Having rough time right now. Enjoy poetry, movies, my cat Spike. Will answer all letters.

/ / /

I am a girl, 15. Just diagnosed and had surgery. I had never heard of it before. I like music and love to dance; take gymnastics. I don't care about your age or anything. Am scared.

/ / /

Single male, 32, from Seattle area. Would like to hear from any female interested in friendship and support. I'm a great listener.

Anne's Colon

After the surgery the surgeon asked Anne's parents if they would like to see Anne's colon. Anne's mother, who had never yet looked away, said, "I couldn't." But her father looked, so he could say what he now says: that Anne is better off without it. He also calls it names, says, "More holes than Swiss cheese," "craters deeper than the moon," "pockmarked," "pitted," "ravaged," "U-G-L-Y."

The surgeon's hands were red and cool. He stood next to a bobbing balloon bouquet and talked to Anne about colons. He said they are inelegant. Big, dumb organs whose agility is limited to spasms of contraction and whose perception of pain is dim and inaccurate.

But Anne thinks of them—of hers—as shy. A mole, maybe. Loathsome, but gentle. A homely animal taken out and shot. And her stomach, her heart, her soul—whatever they've left inside—hurts with the cruelty of it.

Anne and Nicole Shop at the Cosmetic Counter

They are walking past the wooden gleam of a bookstore and a pyramid of soaps, multicolored and clear like Jell-O, in the window of a bath shop.

"I almost fell on the cotillion runway," Nicole says, referring to a time Anne thinks seems as long ago as counting sheep with Bert and Ernie or begging to wear a bra. "Eric gave me his right arm instead of his left, and it threw me off. I kind of wobbled."

"I didn't see a thing," Anne says. She is lying—recalling the gracelessness of it—because what are friends for?

The mannequins have erect nipples but no facial features. A glass elevator rises as if with grace. They walk by Surf, Sea, and Swim where empty bathing suits float disembodied in the blue-tinted display. (Visualize, Anne thinks, a red bikini, sun glistening off the baby oil of an unseamed abdomen.) Escalator teeth endlessly recycle. They hear the patter of the computerized water fountain, brown-bottomed with penny litter. At a table in front of Coffee Breaks, a woman says to a young girl, "But everyone uses a napkin."

"How's Jeff?" Nicole says.

"Fine." Anne makes a face to say, "Like it matters." It's a save-face face, in case she needs it when he comes home.

Nicole says, "I've been feeling ugly as a dog dish. Let's get new makeup."

"I saw this eye shadow that goes on white and changes color in the sun."

"Have you seen that lipstick? Black Ice? It's dark but light at the same time."

They rearrange their bags and retrace their steps, heading for Dillard's cosmetic counter. Anne tries to remember the name of the eye shadow. Glimmer Glow? They pass the movie theater. Nicole points to a coming-soon poster, says while she's kissing she wouldn't mind kissing Johnny Depp. Does Anne happen to have any idea what religion he is?

From the snack bar comes an explosive burst of popcorn, as well as its urgent smell.

"Christian Scientist?" Anne says. "And I think he might also be part Indian."

Nicole grins, as if it's all but done.

In the Music Box Company, someone is trying one out. Anne and Nicole hear the mechanical plunking of "Camptown Races," a tune they do not know.

A Good Paved Road

It's while I'm reading the label on a Rit dye bottle in Osco that I notice Frances Bigelow standing in front of the greeting cards. She's flipped one open—maybe one of those funny cartoon kinds—and tips her head back to read it through her steel-rimmed half-glasses. Her gray hair is held captive by a too-tight perm, but her matching pants, shirt, and vest are a diluted butterscotch. Subtle. An expensive color. One of those handbags like a little suitcase sits in the shopping cart baby seat. She smiles a quick smile of private amusement, tucks the card into an aqua blue envelope, and wheels away, looking pleased and perfectly content ten years after strangers murdered her son in the desert.

It stops me right where I stand. I put the bottle of 003 Pink back on the shelf. The peace of Frances Bigelow's face unnerves me.

At home I say, "Do you remember Frances Bigelow?"

Dennis is parting his hair with a line you could navigate by. Fridays, after Dennis makes a pot of chili, it's bowling with his family. No discussion.

I'm standing in the bathroom door. He says, "Was she in the ward?"

"She's not Mormon."

He slaps his choirboy cheeks with aftershave, checks himself in the mirror, as if it will have made some difference in how he looks.

I say, "Two men shot her son. He was camping with his girlfriend." This was before we were married, but he lived here then, too. "Do you remember? It must be ten years now."

I follow him into the bedroom. He takes his lucky bowling shirt off the hanger, the one with squiggled lines like stenography and a scarlet red yoke on top. His bowling shoes are on the floor, lined up with the bedspread's hem, squared off with the rug's tassels. Toe to toe, heel to heel—at attention. He's thinking, rubs his chin. "I remember the armored truck guy whose body was dropped off at Target."

"No. They raped the girl and then shot the boy, Mrs. Bigelow's son. Did it all in half an hour." *Half* an hour. "He was a good kid. A rich boy, but a Junior Merit Scholar or something like that. In the yearbook picture they put in the newspaper he looked handsome like some forties movie star, with dark wavy hair." It was the wavy hair that had gotten to me, thinking of how he'd probably hated it and tried everything to make it stay flat.

Dennis looks up from his buttoning. "They catch the guys?"

"Yeah, men in their thirties. One of them had been some kind of college athlete. They tried to pawn the boy's class ring. Ended up on death row."

But how much good is that?

I say, "I suppose Mrs. Bigelow's found a way to live with it. Get over it, go on. She looked so normal today."

He tucks in his shirt, a precise clockwise motion starting on his right side. "I'm sure the Lord has sustained her."

"I guess," I say, but it doesn't seem like near enough.

"And ten years is a pretty long time." He puts his shoes in his bag. "Get ready, all you bowling pins."

"They must be shaking in their boots, Dennis." I yank out his shirttail. I have to.

"Aw, Lori," he says, but he's not all that surprised.

/ / /

We take the freeway to his parents' house in Mesa. The Arizona Department of Transportation has decorated the underpasses with giant hieroglyphics, stiff-legged lizards and coiled, intertwined snakes. Probably total gibberish in ancient Indian.

Dennis and I were married last year, two weeks after my twenty-third birthday. I'd been divorced from Lowell for about a year. Lowell was like his name, sweet and slow-moving as your favorite uncle. His skin smelled like a friendly sun.

Dennis clicks off the car radio. He listens to talk radio, or rather he talks to it. "But who in Congress *isn't* under investigation?" he says, getting in the last word. Then to me: "We're putting up the drywall in the house Saturday." He and his father are helping his brother Stan build a house for after he gets married. "Is that OK with you?"

"Yeah, I've got a bunch of errands."

Dennis drives the speed limit. Now he glances at the speedometer. He says that acceleration can sneak up on you like a bad habit.

"You should see Stan picking out lumber," Dennis says. "He sorts through a big old pile of two-by-sixes for a dozen studs. He's such a perfectionist."

"Takes one to know one," I say. "When are we putting in our sprinklers?"

A Greyhound bus passes us on the right. Bright license plates make a patchwork quilt above the bumper.

Dennis frowns, that crease between his eyes. "The only thing is, I haven't decided if we should put bubblers in that planter or drips. Maybe I should pray about it." He's really considering it—praying.

"You'd pray?"

"Yes, talk it over with the Lord."

"Dennis, I don't think he cares."

He looks hurt. "Heavenly Father cares about all of his children."

"Yeah, but their *sprinklers?*"

"I just want to do things right." He hunches over the steering wheel. Dennis talks about Right and Wrong a whole bunch, though he usually doesn't give much explanation about why things are good or bad. He's like those people who say they don't know about art but they know what they like. Dennis is that way with right and wrong; he knows them when he sees them.

We met when he'd been back from his mission three months. Back after preaching night and day for two years in Indiana. At the church dance he talked about it being the best two years of his life, about how he'd learned to love the people of Indiana. How he saw that the Lord had a plan for the people of Indiana. And guess what? Pretty soon it came out the Lord had a plan for me, too. And even though it was as ordinary as marrying Dennis in the Mormon temple, it was what I'd been moving toward all my life, where I would have been anyway, if not for tripping over Lowell's big feet and ending up married to him.

"Will you marry me, Lori, and be my wife for time and all eternity?" Dennis had said, radiant as the angel Gabriel, sure and sweet as a messenger from God should be.

And I said, "Well, sure." Because there it was, a good paved road right at my feet. It was like suddenly figuring out where you are on a map. Direction. The lure of a steady course. You see?

/ / /

Dennis's parents live in a subdivision overrun with red tile roofs and stucco walls. After Doris gets in the car, she drops her bowling bag, *thud,* slams the door, *whump,* before Dennis's dad has even come out of the house. "Hello, sweethearts," she says so cheerfully you know she's got to be furious about something.

When Harry comes out with his head down, I know he's what she's mad at. Before he's even gotten his seat belt fastened, she's said, "When you're your own boss, I think you should be able to get home when you say you will and not always be working."

"Darn it, Doris," he says. "I'm trying. Doing my best."

"It's a pretty poor best," Doris says. "Shoot."

Dennis works for Harry laying tile. Grout under his fingernails, same as mechanic's grease, only white, and his hands pasty as cadavers. He's late a lot, sure, but it doesn't bug me like it does his mom. Lowell was mostly late and early the other way around. Early home, late to work. Switched jobs a lot, had to.

Harry says, "We've got this lady over in Scottsdale who's got it into her head to have mirror tile on the living room floor. Frank's the contractor. He says to give her mirror tile. I say, 'Frank, how about that it'll reflect women's underwear?' 'Her problem,' Frank says. But it's *our* problem when we have to go back in and take it up."

Dennis says, "But Dad can't come right out and mention the underwear thing to her, so he talks about breakage and cleaning upkeep. He can't even look at her. It's like he's thinking she'll think he's talking about *her* underwear."

This gets Doris laughing, then coughing. She's pounding her chest. "Harry," she says, wiping brown tears and mascara clumps off her plump cheeks, "you're such a dopey prude."

Harry says, "Gosh, I know it."

Stan and Jay Lynne already have a lane. They're standing by the beat-up maroon bench signing to each other. Stan is deaf. Jay Lynne thumbs her chin. *Tomorrow,* I think it means. Jay Lynne points to us to let him know we're here.

"You should let me win because I'm older." Dennis speaks to Stan; his signing isn't so hot. What Stan signs back makes Dennis give him a playful punch.

I say hi to Jay Lynne, then finger-spell it to Stan. I make the sign for *I love you.* This is Stan's and my joke because when I met him it was the only sign I knew.

Fair Lanes Bowling Center smells like popcorn and feet—ancient cigarette burns everywhere. The balls sound lopsided rolling down the lanes. By the front door, arcade games are in a glass room. Inside, teenagers compete to look bored.

I put the ball Dennis gave me for Christmas, a green polyester Ebonite, on the rack. It's so substantial it feels like something's on your side.

Doris says, "We're thinking about going to the lake over the long weekend. What do you kids think?" She's turned to Stan so he can read her lips.

"We've got the house to do, Mom," Dennis says. He's pecking out our names on the computer keyboard. His mother scowls. Harry picks up his black plastic ball. *Vengeance,* he calls it. It purrs as it curves toward the pocket, but then goes long.

"Man," he says, after the lonely clunk of only the six and nine pins.

While Jay Lynne takes her turn, Doris pulls a packet of photographs from her huge purse. When Doris isn't telling us about educational TV programs or what happened in her dreams, she's showing us snapshots. "These are from Harry's birthday party," she says.

Their mutt Petey, who looks like a science experiment gone terribly wrong, is in every picture. There's one of Dennis and me in Doris's kitchen eating cake. Petey, wearing a pointed birthday hat, is begging. Behind us is a window ledge loaded with bottles of vitamins and health food remedies.

"We've been picking out the lighting for the house," Jay Lynne says when she sits down. "Harry, do you know the electrician? His name's Roy Bigley."

Dennis says, "Isn't that the name of the boy who got murdered?"

"Bige*low*."

Doris is drying her hands over the blower. "What's this?"

I tell the story, feeling strange. It's the Bigelows' private misery, even though the newspaper told every awful detail. "It was sad," I say at the end, as if that explains it.

Doris adds a fifth step to her delivery and only hits the number ten pin. "That's terrible." Fists on hips, she looks threatening.

Stan signs something with *God* in it, his hand going upward.

I think how brave Frances Bigelow was during the trial. She didn't lean on her corporate executive husband. In fact, she walked a few steps ahead of him in sensible Gucci pumps. She spoke to reporters with some zinging words, so we all knew we were to blame in some way for her loss. "A community is obliged to be responsible for the actions of its most depraved members," she said. But everyone felt too sorry for her to be sore about it.

I was in junior high when it happened. I followed my mother

around asking questions. Would they put the Bigelows on the witness stand? How old did you have to be to watch a trial? Mom flipped on the vacuum cleaner. "Don't know," she said, over its whine. Then, turning it off, "Lori, some things happen in life that are unpleasant. It does no one any good to dwell on them."

"I'm not *dwelling*," I said. "I'm *thinking*. I don't want to get myself killed."

"Go empty the dishwasher," she said. "And stay out of the desert." She meant, I decided later, don't have sex with your boyfriend. She meant, people get what they deserve, sometimes more, sometimes less. Consequences fall into place for my mom, like cards being shuffled. The same as for Dennis. He thinks: eat chocolate, get zits. Go to church, get blessings.

Jay Lynne tugs at a thread on her oxford cloth shirtsleeve. She wears her blond hair in a long ponytail. She looks like everyone else, but I suspect there's something in her past, an addiction or a serious illness. She's not fascinated by suffering. She doesn't ask questions, doesn't express the usual bewilderment. Part of it is how she accepts Stan's hearing loss. Now she pulls up her ball, pauses to rest her chin on it, then dances it to its release—a wild one that surprises us all with its accuracy.

"A strike!" Doris announces.

Confusion seems to erupt with the clatter of the pins. "You lost," crows one of the teenage boys around a Cruising U.S.A. game in the arcade room. A pigtailed girl cries to her mother that last time the mom bought her popcorn *and* Red Vines. Overhead, a voice weary with irritation says, "Will the owner of a green GMC pickup—"

Doris's words interrupt. "Well, how about the lake next weekend?"

/ / /

As we drive home, red lights pulse on the South Mountain broadcast towers. Dennis says, "My mom says bee pollen will cure my allergies."

"Yes, but it'll also give you four extra legs."

He nods like he's weighing it. "And antennas?"

"Two."

"It might not be worth it." He drums his thumbs on the steering wheel.

Ahead a motorcycle cop has stopped a truck pulling a horse trailer. Dennis nods, reassured by this evidence of where going too fast gets you. The bumper sticker on the Honda in front of us says, "WELCOME TO ARIZONA. NOW GO HOME."

I say, "How about Jay Lynne's strike?"

"She's getting better," Dennis says. He glances at the side mirror. "You know, sometimes I'm a little worried about Stan and her. It's hard to get used to living with someone with all that quiet." He waves his arm as if to break up the stillness.

"It's funny, I don't think of him as quiet."

"He doesn't turn on a radio or the TV. He doesn't even hum to himself. It can get to you. I just hope she knows what she's in for."

"Oh," I say, not really thinking about Jay Lynne, but about the things I've gotten into myself. Like Lowell, thinking again about Lowell. How he cleared his throat before he lied. How he nicked the mole on his chin shaving. That there was a white V tan line by his toes from wearing flip-flops everywhere.

I remember him lying on his back in our patchy Bermuda grass wearing a black T-shirt with a hole by the neck where chest hair stuck out. "Lori," he called, "it's almost time." He jiggled his foot so his flip-flop wagged. "Ouch." He slapped an ant on his arm. "There, look." They swooped out of this house thing he'd made for them. Bats. Dark and small, so fast they appeared to be the blur of animated outlines. They flew around the mulberry tree like a nursery rhyme. Then about five of them skimmed the water in the rusty barbecue. Their flight was only a few feet above my head. But it was like an adventure, watching their climb into a faded orange sunset striped with smoky lavender clouds.

I said, "You're sure they're not just birds?"

"Hell, no. Brown bats. They wash themselves like cats. Every night they can eat up to half their weight in insects. Happy hunting," he yelled, getting to his feet as the bats scattered. "Curfew at dawn." He took off his T-shirt and waved the bats on. "It's like a launching," he explained.

"Or buddies going out drinking?"

"Yeah," he said, liking that, as usual missing the connection to *his* occasional outings.

The last bat flew low over the grapefruit tree we'd planted. Its flight was more irregular, I saw then, than a bird's. A rush of energy that was somehow calming.

"Who eats the bats?" I said.

"What?" Lowell tossed his T-shirt toward the house.

"The bats. They eat insects. Who eats *them?*"

Slowly, he scratched his chest. "Owls." He had gentle-looking hands, soft like a dentist's. "Hawks." He shoved his hands in his pockets until his jeans sagged in front. When he stepped toward me I began to lose track of my point about being eaten. Something about Lowell's job and reminding him to look over his shoulder. Big fish eat little fish, and worse, was my point.

"Snakes," he added, holding on to the *s*. From Lowell, talk of predators seemed remote, unlikely. It was impossible to feel the harm of them, even to the bats.

"Bats," he whispered into my hair, "out for a good time."

"After the good time?" I struggled to say.

"More good times." A kiss—a long one because Lowell was never in a rush, particularly in his pleasures.

And that was the direction things often took with Lowell. My complaints and warnings were never much noted. He *enjoyed* things: bats or the design of bullet-proof vests or the vexing question of why Buddy Ryan couldn't make anything of the Cardinals' offense. He was content. For Lowell, everything was for now. No questions asked, no plans made. But that was what eventually got to me, what I couldn't take. What about the rent next month, Lowell? What if you've got pneumonia, Lowell? What if. . . . But he kissed away discussion and left me with my worries—thick and dull, soaring himself into some colorful, slowing fading sky.

/ / /

Saturday morning Harry is here before I've gotten dressed. He's pinching the broken zipper tab on a gray hooded sweatshirt. He says, "It'll be a long José day." But I know that's what he's hoping. He's looking forward to that work.

Harry and Dennis want to lend a hand, beg to. When the ward puts on a widow's new roof, they're the first ones there. Move-ins, move-outs. It's Harry and Dennis. They clean eggs at the welfare farm and can tomato sauce at the cannery. "By love serve one another." Galatians 5:13

"We meeting Stan there?" Dennis says.

"He's getting the Sheetrock."

Dennis grabs his black lunch box and kisses me. "Maybe we can catch a movie tonight."

I go to Osco to get some aspirin and shoelaces, but it's the greeting cards I end up at. They line both sides of aisle four with their weirdly specific divisions. MOM FROM BOTH, WIFE-RELIGIOUS, and the best: OH, LOVE IS STILL BEAUTIFUL. There are some blurry photographs of boats on quiet waters and red poppies standing in fields, but mostly cartoons by where Mrs. Bigelow was standing, between the FUN AT WORK and BEST FRIENDS markers.

After the trial she and her husband divorced, though I'd heard my mother say to her friend Sister Marcus that she'd never seen a man as supportive as Mr. Bigelow. "Right by her side," she said. But Sister Marcus said, "Oh, but think of the grief! How could a marriage take that? How could anyone?"

And that's what I wanted to know. Later, I'd see her sometimes in the newspaper's Life section. She'd be looking over another woman's shoulder at something a group of them were holding, a service award or an art object to be auctioned. But she looked different from the others. Her nose had a hump. Her face was old and drooped, not old and tight. She looked less *society,* more PTA, or Mormon Relief Society, for that matter. Ordinary-looking, like Sister Marcus or my mother, but wearing Biltmore Fashion Park clothes.

Kathleen with the white Dragon Lady fingernails is on check-out at Osco. She says, "Did you find everything you need, hon?"

"Sure," I say, then on a hunch, "Kathleen, do you know Frances Bigelow?"

"Does she work here or something?"

"No, she's just a customer."

Kathleen rings up the sale with a pencil eraser. "Nope, never heard of her. Three dollars and sixteen cents. Have a really good day for me." She flips down the black bar that separates people's purchases.

When Dennis comes home, he's covered with drywall dust. "Stan and Jay Lynne are putting carpet in most of the rooms," he says. When he sighs, I think there's a white puff of drywall dust. "Dad and I told them we could tile it for half the cost, but Stan said carpet was softer. *And* quieter." He looks dejected as he unlaces his work boots. His bare feet are pale, the only part of him not dusty. Jesus' feet. He wiggles his toes. "I'm so tired," he says.

I go to the kitchen while he showers, admiring this about him, that he works hard, will see a job to the end. I cook some hamburger for tacos, wondering if when I have children I'll compare them to each other like I compare my husbands. Lowell I think of as I chop onions, and how he explained quitting work for Doug Howell, then Steve Williams, and later, both Mr. Sears and Mr. Roebuck.

I did trip over Lowell's feet, literally, in world history at Coronado High School, his long legs, too, crossed at the ankle, sticking out in the aisle. I stumbled and fell. And without getting up and without particular urgency, he caught me, smooth and practiced, as if he sat all day every day in this too-small desk for just this purpose. There was no laughter in his face; neither was there apology. Concern? Puppy love? No, neither. There was what there always was: a certain pleased interest.

"Did you have a nice trip?" he said, pulling me back up.

"Just wished you could have gone," I said.

He grinned. Lowell lived his life like he was watching it in a movie. He was always plenty entertained by it, but it wasn't anything he was going to get sweaty or silly over.

"We'll have to do it again sometime," he said, like the gentleman he always was.

"Sometime," I'd said, trying for the right combination of flirtation and indifference, but wanting something from him even then, something more than just boy and girl.

Dennis says the blessing on the food, praying that we use the energy derived from it to do good. He reaches for the taco sauce. He'll pour a huge pool of it to dip his taco in. Does the same with the syrup for waffles, ketchup for hamburgers.

"So did it hurt your dad's feelings about them wanting carpet?"

"Well, you know you can just keep tile cleaner, and it wears so much better." He's been thinking about this in the shower, lathering up with it.

I say, "But, you know, if it's what they want."

"But I'd like to help them avoid costly mistakes."

His conviction that mistakes can be avoided amazes me—as does his confidence in identifying them.

"Making mistakes is the best way to learn," I say, something I've heard somewhere before—church or a women's magazine.

Dennis pours his taco sauce lake. "They should just listen, is all," he says, sulky but ready to give it up.

I consider the carpet Stan and Jay Lynne will choose. A tight weave, something subdued and practical, gray or beige. It will swallow sound, muffle disagreement. A buffer. A cocoon. Peace. But suddenly I hunger for the sharp protest of a drinking glass dropped on tile, a noise to make you catch your breath and notice, and I remember Dennis saying how quiet can get to you, that it can start to be too much.

/ / /

We sit on a middle bench in sacrament meeting the next day. The missionaries in front of us have an investigator with them, someone they're trying to convert—a large woman with a dainty face who smells of cigarettes. On the stand, a lacy tablecloth covers the sacrament table. Behind it, teenage priests cradle their heads in their hands. Organ pipes cover the wall behind the choir seats, like rows of obedient whistles.

The first time I took Lowell to church he whispered, "Where's the cross?"

"Don't have them," I whispered back.

"Enjoy a cross," he said, "always find them stirring."

The speaker is a new member of the ward. She's talking about faith, Peter walking on the water and all. Dennis is getting into it. I think he's really some kind of Born Again, disguised as a Mormon. He'd love to shout *Amen, sister* and *Praise the Lord* in the middle of the meeting. I'm sure it's stifling for his amens to be confined the way they are, just mumbled at the ends of prayers and talks. The speaker's words are complete little worlds themselves, every consonant pronounced distinctly. She quotes, "Now faith is the substance of things hoped for, the evidence of things not seen." And before she can say it, Dennis whispers to me, "Hebrews 11:1." The investigator turns and looks at him. The skin on her neck twists like an ancient tortoise's.

The missionaries tried to convert Lowell. At the end of their discussions he would say, "Isn't that interesting?" The missionaries encouraged him to pray for guidance. He had, he said, and the Spirit spoke to him about tolerance and individuality. I knew then that the missionaries were licked, but I knew I was, too. Not because Lowell wasn't going to be a Mormon, but because he couldn't see that it even mattered. This became clear: I was planning for eternal life; Lowell was looking forward to the weekend.

The speaker adjusts the microphone closer to her mouth, as if what she's about to say is a secret just for us. "I quote from the great prophet Alma," she says, and Dennis opens his Book of Mormon to follow along. His sharply parted hair falls into his eyes.

I lean over. "I'm not feeling well. I'm going home."

He squints in concern. "I'll take you."

"No, I can drive."

He moves his legs aside to let me by. "I'll get Brother Richards to take me home. Feel better."

The investigator turns and smiles timidly as I leave.

/ / /

When Lowell answers the door, he doesn't look surprised. "Hi, Lor," he says, like I still live here and have forgotten my key to this small house with gravel for a front yard, a snaky ocotillo, and a saguaro that too many cactus wrens have pecked on and lived in. He opens the torn screen door, nods me in.

"I'm ditching church, Lowell."

He says, "I always thought you were overdoing that church thing." He has the posture for harmonica playing—the glides and slides—but the sadness wouldn't stick, I think. Couldn't.

"I've been missing you," I say, because it is true.

His shrug. "Leaving was your choice." True, as well.

We've walked through the house, out the back door, past the round terra-cotta thermometer. I was the one who put it up, with its pheasants flying over the 50- and 80-degree marks. Lowell sits on the grass. He rarely sits on chairs.

I say, "How have you been?"

"You know what? I've joined this volunteer group that puts up playgrounds for needy children. The big wood kind. You should see the kids when we get them done." There is a chicken pox scar under his eye. How familiar it is shocks me—as well as the crust of dried blood on the mole on his chin. "I love it when the kids tell me things in Spanish."

"You understand them?"

"Spanish?" He smiles, happy with the thought of a Spanish-speaking Lowell.

Under the hulking box of the room air conditioner is a vegetable garden. The tomatoes are orange. Young carrots grow like a row of little ferns. Behind is the bat house, still there, nailed to a post like a country mailbox.

"How are the bats?" I say.

Lowell stands and looks up, as if he's watching a bat flying past its morning bedtime.

"I was remembering the other day how you used to say they were moths or birds. 'Swallows,' you said. I'd point out how they fly different from birds. Their muscles are on their chests and backs. They pull themselves through the air like a swimmer's butterfly stroke."

"Yes, bats." I pronounce it like the speaker in church, precisely, giving it a clear ending. I look at the house thing filled, I guess, with sleeping bats.

Lowell says, "Can I get you something to drink? How about a beer?" He smiles mischievously.

"Oh, no, Lowell."

"Just wanted to see how far you'd fallen. How about something to eat?"

"No thanks."

He puts his hands into his pockets.

I wonder if he has enough money. I wonder if he's been hurt by my leaving. Does he have a girlfriend? Does she appreciate what he is? Or is not? Is he happy? Will he be all right?

My knees feel wobbly like I drank that beer. With my thumb, I wipe the dried blood off his chin. I say, "Lowell, how are you doing?" It is an urgent question about what has happened: what he has done and what I have done. A question about the past and what comes now.

He smiles. First his cheek dimples, next his lips twitch, then I see his teeth with their slight overlap in the front like a kiss. A slow smile, of course, a take-your-time smile.

Victor's Funeral Urn

A reporter accosts me outside of Safeway and asks how I feel about mayonnaise. His tan looks baked and smooth as enamel. His yellow tie is jaunty, purchased with promotion in mind.

"Ma'am," he says, sober as a police lineup, "excuse me. Can you give us a moment? And tell us, if you will, what is it you want from your mayonnaise?"

This is what's wrong with the world: we think everything is important. I've wheeled my shopping cart only as far as the jeep I've parked next to. Among the litter on its floor I see an orthodontic headgear and a Land Rover hood ornament.

Mayonnaise. Posed this way, abruptly and from a member of the media, the question does sound like it matters—what with the cameraman recording me for immediate broadcast on the six o'clock news. Now I'm the one feeling stupid, like I should have been giving mayonnaise more consideration. After I exclaim my earnest answer, the reporter leaves me quick and bored as a one-night stand.

It's while I'm driving home that I realize I sounded patriotic. Besides, I never say just one stupid thing when two will do. It relieves me to know my twelve-year-old son Max has never watched the news. And my ex-husband, a commercial developer, will be cocooned in a lacewood-paneled conference room. He'll be talking about square-foot rentals, unaware that his ex-wife is acting the fool.

The sky is the moist gray that usually burns off earlier. Six years in La Jolla, I still insist Californians must be born knowing how to drive. I imagine them in baby walkers shaped like automobiles. I grew up in the Midwest, where driving was a cautiously acquired skill. The traffic creeps on Ocean Boulevard, all the way to the turnoff for a worn-out bungalow I'm selling—or trying to.

I put my Open House sign in the trunk and notice in the fading light the house doesn't look so pitiful. A nice touch: the front porch is deep and shaded by bougainvillea in brilliant red bloom. *A little paint is all,* that's what I'll be saying. *Paint,* real estate's magic word.

Then I see the urn in the gutter. It's with some child's school papers. *Circle the hard g sounds,* the instructions say. There is an early reader, *Ernest Otter's Escape.* The urn itself is on its side, dented like a can on the quick sale shelf—pewter with a shape like a car racing trophy.

Victor Anthony Mendia-Flores. His birth date and his death, a little less than two years apart.

I decide to take it home with me. How do I explain that? I can see a young girl in an orange clown wig dancing in a neighboring house's front window. But I don't knock. On the way home, I ease into the fast lane. I say, "Victor, I'm going to find where you belong."

At the condo, son Max and his friend Austin are sitting on bar stools in front of tacos. Austin is exclaiming over his fish taco. He quotes his mother, who says she wouldn't eat anything from the garbage dump ocean. Clearly, his delight in his food is enhanced by her disgust. As I struggle in with a torn grocery bag and the urn clamped under my arm, Max puts down his taco and comes toward me. I expect him to take the bag, but instead he stops and says, "What am I going to do tomorrow?" His voice creaks on *going*.

Austin wipes his hands on his pants, waves uncertainly, blurts, "It gives a sandwich meaning? Mayonnaise does?" He nods several times, as if he wants to agree.

Max sits down, puts his head on his folded arms. From the refrigerator there's the clattering of tumbling ice cubes. Max's Eddie Bauer backpack slumps against the answering machine that is indicating five calls.

"Look," I say, "I'm sorry." I remember when it started happening, this great leveling of mother and son. When last year, just before the divorce, Max glimpsed behind the *Wizard of Oz* curtain—behind the booming voice demanding bedroom cleaning and teeth brushing—and saw the puny reality of me. And how could he hide his disappointment? How could he pretend anything would ever be the same?

"Max," I say, "no one you know watches the six o'clock news."

"Unless their school is on it for collecting food for the homeless." His sneakers squeak his protest on the oak floor all the way to his room.

Austin rubs his mouth vigorously with a paper napkin and picks up the domed pepper mill, says, "Ah, he's just mad."

Max is a perfectionist, a child who would tear up the picture he was coloring if he went out of the lines. *That's great*, I learned to say about everything, and Max would always counter with just where a particular project hadn't gone right.

Austin tells me how many cans they collected and how it means they get out of school early. He's a kid you could only call scruffy, with an underdog-lover, cat-in-a-tree-rescuer kind of face. I'm sure he didn't worry much about coloring.

"Want some milk?" I say before I put it away. I'm hoping the exasperated hum from the refrigerator isn't as important as it sounds, when Austin says of the funeral urn, "What's that?" He reaches for it.

"I found it," I say. "A funeral urn."

He recoils and smiles sheepishly. "Are you keeping it?"

"I have to find its parents. It—he—was just a baby. The urn was lying in the street."

"I hope it isn't a bomb," Max says, back standing in the doorway. "Why don't you call the police?"

Which is actually what I do, but not then, not for a while.

/ / /

Surely divorce is the most public of failures. Untidy, personal, inevitable—a hair clog in a bathroom sink. And this is the thing with my marriage, it could have been saved if I'd been willing. Lee and I would still be married if I had been able to forgive. It is the truest thing I know.

He came to me himself about his affair, tears in his eyes. Why tears? I wondered, even after he told me. Amid this crushing shock, a curious question: what about guilt makes someone weep? Oh, he'd broken it off. He said, "I've been terribly mistaken." He said, "Maureen, I love you. I know that now."

I knew he was a liar in little ways, understating his golf handicap or in a story of a dispute with a contractor, reporting he'd said what he only wished he had. But this. How could I ever trust anything? And where was the intuition a wife was supposed to have? I couldn't think of a single unaccounted-for absence, and then I couldn't think of a single absence that didn't seem suspect.

"You're a Mormon," I'd said when he told me, not mad like I thought women were when something like this happened, but scared, shaking, guessing life as I knew it—charity work, lunches, lovemaking, homemaking—was over. We were in the bathroom. The mirrors were steamed from my shower. I was clutching the mascara wand like a weapon. Defense. It trembled in my hand.

Lee said, "I *was* a Mormon." He'd told me years before how his real name, Helaman, came from the Book of Mormon. A general who led two thousand young men into battle and returned them to their mothers without one of them getting killed. How his parents had taught him about sinning. "Mormonism," he said, "has lots of commandments. It's like Puritanism squared."

"But being a Mormon, or having been a Mormon, how do you feel having done this?"

"That's why I told you, Maureen. I wanted us to have a fresh start," he said.

"Are there fresh starts for something like this?" Smoke damage, I thought. How your belongings might be untouched by fire, but how you'd never get out the campfire stink.

I *knew* Lee, how he'd always order salmon if it were on the menu, but not if I'd ordered it first. I knew how he'd let a dog lick his face, or ask a stranger to save his place in line. But suddenly I didn't know him at all. The father of my child, who when he helped with homework had always said, "The answer is upstairs!" and tapped his own head with the pencil eraser before he crossed his eyes.

"We can go on. I want to," he said. "It's up to you."

Why should this have landed in my lap? I hadn't done anything wrong. Then I decided I *must* have been guilty, and I remembered a thousand selfish crimes. They floated to me unbidden as I tried to sleep, as I listened to Lee's breathing. Sometimes he seemed to snore an apology, sometimes he exhaled without regret. I'd struggle with questions of who knew about his affair, as I sat at the kitchen table making a house out of sugar cubes, my fingers sticky and sad. I ate sunflower seeds. There is revenge in salt. I'd think how this meant I wouldn't be remodeling the kitchen, which seemed not a loss of convenience and luxury, but of the future itself, now shoe box–sized.

I thought of telling his family, calling up his parents in Utah, after they'd come home from church. His dad would be putting his scriptures on the kitchen counter as the phone rang. He'd call, "Mother, Maureen has something to say." They would be on my side.

But one day as I told Judith Long I couldn't do collections for Clean Air California, I thought, what's the good of being on the right side of this? Does the high moral ground leave me any more whole? Weeks went by. I got thin, then fat, until the therapist slapped down her notepad, insisted I repeat, "My happiness is up to me."

Returning from her office, I knocked the side mirror off the Mercedes coming into the garage. Lee was in the bedroom doing a crossword puzzle. He never did crossword puzzles, but I did, and I hadn't because I'd lost the ability to concentrate. I hated him thoroughly just for that.

"Get out of here!" I screamed. "You cheat, and I pay. Enough!" I felt light and instantly peaceful. The atmosphere seemed somehow depleted but serene.

Lee put down the newspaper and walked out of the room. All he said was, "I understand."

/ / /

In the evening after friends call to comment on my philosophy of mayonnaise: "creative," "enlightened," "crazy, but brave," I go to check on Max. He's reading his book, *God Is My Co-pilot,* an unsettling title if ever there was one. His hobby and obsession is World War II fighter planes, a passion he shares with his father, a passion about which he is noticeably more passionate since his father moved out. On the wall is a poster: a P-51—its nose an astonishing mustard color—is shooting down an evil-looking ME-109. Their archaic menace is daunting. Once when I asked Max why he liked fighters, he said, "It was the last one-on-one combat. Win or lose. Live or die." It left me dismayed and worried, proved completely how he would someday move beyond my reach.

Now he is lying on his bed in boxer shorts. They are dotted with basketballs and cocky purple Lakers' insignia. The hair of his legs is turning darker. His shoulders seem to have broadened, which oddly makes him look more vulnerable, instead of less. Even at rest, his body is a coil of impatience.

"I've got a science test tomorrow," he says, "pulsar, quasar, star constellations."

Suddenly the sting of memory: lying on our bed, through the window streaks of sun so insouciant I know I'll learn to take California for granted. Lee and I identifying freckle constellations on the giggling, delighted Max. "I swear, Cassiopeia," Lee says, and I say, "Now, Max, lie still and let Mother see." It fills me with a yearning that makes me look now at my empty hands, remembering the soft warmth of his young skin and the sharp juts of elbow and knee. A moment too ordinary to remember, but there it is, tinged now with the grief of what came later.

"Have you studied for your test?" I say, though I know he has and now almost wish he hadn't. It occurs to me that someone who would let himself off the hook occasionally might also let me.

"Yep," he says, "read the chapter, twice."

Sometimes I'll run across an E-mail he's sending. (His online name is Mustang. "Oh, Mother, it's the fighter, not the car.") There's a lightness to it I wouldn't have thought him capable of—a humor that is in fact funny. I'm as amazed as I'll be the day he grows a beard. Once I heard him say on the phone, "Let's not get there before the babes." And I thought of infants. Really, for a minute I didn't know what he could mean. Almost everything about motherhood has surprised me, every moment so much stranger or more wonderful than what has come before.

"Sorry about the mayonnaise stuff, Max. I guess I didn't think."

"Oh, you couldn't help it," he says, with a forgiveness and a hopelessness that suggest I am a disaster, a lava-spewing volcano or a tree-churning tidal wave. I can't help the damage I cause.

"Maybe your friends didn't recognize me."

"Yeah, they did." As if my television debut is something the whole seventh grade has been watching for. Then a shift: "Dad's talking about taking me to see Grandpa and Grammy in Utah. Is that OK?"

I see in his eyes how unpredictable I am. How I would deny a boy a trip to see his grandparents. "Probably," I say, "depends on school, doesn't it?"

"Yeah." He shuts his book, a thud that sounds resigned and discouraged. The F-14 Tomcat hanging from the ceiling takes a dispirited flight on an open-window breeze. "I knew you wouldn't just say yes."

"But when is it?"

"What do you care?"

"Oh, Max. Let's not be like this."

"I'm not being like anything."

"Max?"

"Just goodnight."

"I'll talk to your dad." But he's already turned over. A brooding mound facing another poster, this one of a Japanese fighter, its nose skyward.

/ / /

At least 75 percent of the divorced women I know are selling houses or doing interior design for them. Trying to work through the failures in their own homes, is what I always think. Homemakers still trying to make homes. I'm guilty, I'll admit it. I drive the impossible Mercedes I got in the settlement, a 560SL—a car too expensive to keep, too intimidating to sell—in these days when I'm doing my own cleaning and selling strangers' houses to strangers. Learning secrets they don't even know they have. The homeowner makes unwitting confessions. Twin beds in the master bedroom. Piles of newspapers against a wall. You don't have to look in drawers to know people's stories. They seem to have forgotten they even have stories to tell.

The best or the most alarming: the day coming up from a wood shop in a basement when my client and I noticed blood drops on the stairs.

/ / /

I put it in the *San Diego Tribune:*
Found: funeral urn. Inscribed Victor Anthony Mendia-Flores. Call evenings, Maureen. 498-6775

/ / /

No one calls, just Lee, asking about taking Max to Utah. "The weekend after next," he says. "It's not my turn." Apology in his voice for this, for everything.

Max told me Lee's been reading the Book of Mormon and telling him about repentance—the four *R*s. Max said, "You're supposed to recognize your mistake, have remorse for committing it, make restitution to the person you hurt, resolve to never do it again." He ticked them off on his fingers, ending with a wagging baby finger. "Right," I said, rolling the *r* and wondering what restitution you make for betrayal.

To Lee on the phone: "That'll be fine. Max is looking forward to it."

"Great," he says. Set free of the constraint of my giving trouble, he's really pleased. And the part of me I hate but can't let go of instantly regrets I've made him so glad.

Afterward, I go to the balcony, sit in a white wicker chair with my legs tucked under me, and take solace in the monotony of the sea. I don't have enough money to replace the refrigerator, but the condo Lee and I bought together has a pricey ocean view. On the beach, a man in a windbreaker navigates around some mounds of translucent brown kelp. He tosses a white Frisbee into the waves, which bobs faithfully back. He snaps his wrist and the Frisbee spins farther out before its banking, inevitable drop. I'd like to be free of my anger at Lee, released from its weight and direction. I'd be like I was before, before the thought of his infidelity became something small, dependable, and hard.

And I wonder what was true in all he told me. He seems to me now completely unknowable, the hidden crevices of his soul hidden from him as well. What does he think, really, of his behavior? Has he let himself off as easily as it seems?

"Hey," Max says behind the screen door. Austin stands by him, a remote control of some kind still in his hand. "Could Austin and me make a sandwich?" Then a mischievous gleam just before he laughs at this: "He can't wait to try our mayonnaise."

/ / /

I go back to the neighborhood where I found the urn. I check with the mailman. Phone calls using my bad Spanish. *Tiene. Muerte. Usted sabe?* One woman starts yelling curses. Another tells me that her baby was kidnapped thirty years ago in Juarez.

Max says, "It's like something that couldn't be lost. I mean, how could it?"

"I think it fell when someone was moving. Like out of a pickup truck," I say.

"But you'd stop and get it." Then I see it occur to him it could fall out without someone noticing. "You'd find it. Wouldn't you?" He rubs at a spot of eczema on his arm. I've put ointment on those patches so many times when he was younger, it's as if I know the itchy heat of how it feels. "Mom," he says, "I mean, you'd get it back?"

"Of course," I say. "I'd drive like a maniac." And I wonder if this isn't really about his father and me.

"Yeah." He registers doubtful relief. I remember how when we told him about the divorce his reaction was physical. He flung his arm and shut his eyes. He slumped, as if from a blow. His actions surprised me, though not the intensity. I'd expected him to suffer, but I didn't expect his rejection of us with the hurt.

Restless, I turn back to the phone, but I'm at the end of the calls.

Max says, "For now, we'll have to keep him."

I follow him into the den and watch as he puts the urn on the coffee table, moves aside an art book on gargoyles and a lucky ringed stone he found on the beach. We stand back with satisfaction, as if we've given Victor shelter from a storm.

From then on we start to become aware of the urn's presence, as if it's a seance spirit or a troubled conscience. When the TV advises viewer discretion, I weigh whether or not Max should be watching, while Max gets up and turns the urn's inscription to the wall. And when a heroic space traveler shoots a sleek, lizardy creature, Max yells, "Victor, did you see *that?*" Always during commercials we talk about Victor and what he might have been like.

We wonder how many words he spoke. We hope he was bilingual. Max says, "Was he in diapers?" "Do you think he was chubby?" He adds, "I bet he liked Barney. We should leave that on sometimes for him."

Max says, "It's just lucky for him that we found him."

And for some reason I don't understand, I agree it surely is.

/ / /

Standing in the door Lee says, "Max says you have a body."

It shocks me put that way, but so does the unexpected appearance of Lee. He usually waits for Max in the car. He's wearing a shirt without a collar, a shirt that says to me, *Look at me, how well I'm moving on.* I think he looks like his brother, then I realize he looks like Max—the same crease of the upper lip, the elongated eye-shape—slightly exotic—a partial shrug now of one shoulder.

"I found it," I say of the urn, as if it's an answer.

He ducks his head to walk through the door, though he walked through it a million times when he lived here and never once bumped.

"In here," Max says, leading his father into the den, then shoving the urn toward him.

Lee takes it. He's wearing a green shirt with blue slacks. He's color-blind and didn't ask the clerk the new shirt's color. His color mistakes used to touch me like a kid with his shoes on the wrong feet. He turns from the urn to me, raises an eyebrow. A look I recognize, a look of concern. He says, "Can I help you find its home? I mean, its owners. I could make some calls." He puts his finger into the dent. "Man, how does something like this happen?"

"I'll take care of it," I say, feeling like I've failed something. Or like I've shoplifted.

Max says, "We like it." And maybe for the first time I realize, I'm keeping someone's ashes.

Lee puts the urn back on the table. His hair is cut differently, which makes me suddenly know he has a girlfriend. I am quicker on such clues now that it is no longer my concern. Is this what I got from marriage?

The wallpaper is cranberry-colored string cloth. There is a

lithograph with bright intersecting squares. Lee says, almost to himself, "There are probably laws against keeping it." Then to me, "What do you think?"

"I think," I say, with a calmness so tough it has no openings, "that it is entirely none of your business."

He says, "Ready, Max?"

But Max has heard it, understands the ugliness of the exchange. I remember a friend who told me of her surprise at the divorce of her parents, how she didn't expect it because they never fought. When she got older she realized *that* was exactly the trouble. Max knows in the old days we would have countered back and forth with *what-do-you-mean?* He looks at the urn so as not to face our hot indifference.

He says, "I'm ready." He turns to me. "You don't need to wait up."

"Goodnight, Maureen," Lee says with wonderful civility, reminding me that starting out on the wrong side doesn't necessarily mean you'll lose.

/ / /

Then I call the police. To the local precinct I say, "I've found a body."

"Address?" the woman barks.

I see how it sounds. "I meant, I've found ashes."

Quiet on the line, then, "Ma'am, how do you know they're human?"

After some holding, my explanation lands me with a Detective Nolan, a noisy breather who seems completely perplexed. "I'll check birth and death records," he offers. "Why don't you bring the urn in?"

"Please," I say to the policeman, "just look. OK? I'll keep it here. I want it to be safe."

When Max comes home, I ask about the concert. He says, "All that music Dad likes sounds the same to me." He sits on my bed and seems to wait, as if I've called him here, patient as if there's something *I* want to say. With a finger he traces the flowers on my comforter, one after the other—and the whole thing is flowers: tulips, daisies, roses. The care he takes in doing it in some way breaks my heart. Finally he says, "I'm scared something bad happened to Victor. They wouldn't have just left him there if he was someone people loved."

I reach for his arm and squeeze it. "Max, I'm not sure what happened to Victor. I hope it wasn't something really bad." But, of course, babies don't die happily and sadness settles in the room.

Max says, "If you repent, you can be forgiven. You see, it's like a big eraser. Gone. It's like it never happened."

"Yes, I see," I say to stop him, but it doesn't. And again he tells me how to make mistakes right.

/ / /

After we were married, our first house was a trailer. The floor sloped from the living room to the bedroom. When we passed in the hall we always kissed, because we couldn't pass without touching and also because we were young. For our first anniversary Lee gave me a used washer and dryer, which he was delighted with because he'd found them himself and because he thought they were the color I wanted, a new appliance color: almond. They were gold. A definite out-of-date gold. I remember him taking them out of his friend's truck, the two of them wrestling the ugly machines to the ground. And his smile, his smile of genuine pleasure. I made myself a promise, and I kept it. I never told him they were gold.

/ / /

I've found this house for a pastry chef, perfect, small as, in fact, a cake. A house so tiny that even San Diego outside the window begins to look reduced. I'm baffled when he says, "What about the dampness?"

"The dampness?"

"Living so close to the ocean, won't everything rust?"

I think of how my career and my new refrigerator need this sale. I think how I was trained to "downplay frivolous concerns." But I say, "This close to the ocean, everything rusts, unless it mildews. No, sometimes both." For some reason, my honesty makes him relax. He's older. He's told me about the career opportunities he's passed by because he likes to focus on the miniature precision of a Napoleon or a linzertorte. Now he stands and looks out the window toward the ocean, which is really at least two miles away.

My beeper buzzes. Detective Nolan's number appears on the display.

When I drop off the chef, he says he will consider it. "After a while one wants a house, an abode of one's own." He's red-headed, densely freckled, rusted-looking himself. He repeats *abode* in a way that sounds cozy.

From my office I give Detective Nolan a call.

"Illegitimate," he says. "Mexican national. Father imprisoned on felony charges." Computer keys clicking. "Grand theft, auto; aggravated assault."

"His mother?"

"Guadalajara—no, wait, that's her mother lives there. The mother herself, is—wow—apparently incarcerated also. Drug charges. Some home life, huh?"

"What about Victor?" I feel out of focus. For a moment, I've forgotten he's already dead.

Detective Nolan says, "His birth's in the file, but nothing about his death. Doesn't mention it."

I'm stunned as if I'd known them, as if I've watched the squalor of crime and poverty defeat his life. I rest my head on my desk. There is peace in its battered wood.

"The remains," I say.

"You'd better bring them in."

/ / /

I go to his room while Max is packing to go to Utah. He has a tower of clothing on his bed.

"Max," I say, "it's only for a few days."

"I don't know what people wear in Utah." He whines this. It's always a challenge, this effort to look exactly like everyone else. "Grandpa might take me fishing. And there's an Air Force base we get to visit." Saying that, he seems to remember he's going on vacation. The tension gives way to a look of anticipation. I wonder then if I should tell him about Victor. I take out some boxers and open the closet for a jacket. There's neatness in his closet. It's so precise—even military—for a moment I can't stand the sight.

"Max, I got a call back from the police about Victor. They've found his parents."

"Where are they?"

"They're in prison." I rush on, to get it over. The child we'd imagined together is materializing in a harsh true light. "They don't know what happened to Victor. They found his birth record but nothing about his death."

"It probably wasn't even reported," Max says, with a cynicism a boy shouldn't have. He shoves some of his clothes into a duffel bag. He moves the bag and slouches down on the bed. Around the room the various flyers are frozen in action, the action of being killed or killing, man's most ancient purpose or plight.

"I have to take the urn to the police station. Now that they've found the parents, we have to return it."

"Return what? Victor?"

"His ashes."

"But that's all that's left of him." A scornful laugh. He stands up and flings an arm toward the window, as if it's some sort of explanation of his distress. "I've just been waiting for this to happen," he says. And when he says it, I know that he has.

"Max."

"This is about me going to Utah with Dad, isn't it?"

"What?"

"You wouldn't be doing this if I weren't going with Dad."

"This has nothing to do with Dad, Max." Trying to be calm, I say, "This is about Victor."

He sneers. "It's the same thing. They both got kicked out."

Why does this surprise me? Why does it leave me feeling frightened and cold? Numbly I move toward him. "Max, that's not how it happened."

He backs up and we stand there, mother and son, in this room just another set of combatants with weapons as deadly and wounds of the soul.

/ / /

Though he won't speak to me, that night I dream of Max on the beach, throwing handfuls of sand into the ocean. Throwing and throwing until it seems the ocean would be full. Then I realize it's not sand, but Victor's ashes.

/ / /

After Lee and Max leave for Utah, I find the urn is missing. It doesn't surprise me, but it fills me with a still, deep sorrow. I hear my conversation with Detective Nolan: my strange confession that the urn is gone.

I call the grandparents' number. Lee's father answers. A friendly voice, it makes me feel less anxious.

"It's me, George, Maureen."

"Why, Maureen," he says, as if it's really a pleasure. I wish, suddenly, my kindness ran that deep.

"May I speak to Max or maybe Lee?"

"Which one?" he says, in his gentle Rocky Mountain drawl.

Then an explosion of panic like the time I lost Max in the grocery store. The running up and down aisles, the quick, senseless bargains with God. "Are they there?" I say in a frozen whisper. "George, they're there, aren't they?"

Soothing, grandfatherly answer: "They're right here. Everyone here, hon, but you."

Pruitt Love

Holly had lank blond hair, eyebrows transparent as canola oil, and a standard face. A regular face. Neil told her that, the part about her face, actually blurted it on their second date. After he walked her to her apartment door, where he was possibly—probably—supposed to be doing something suave and bold that involved hands/mouths and skilled movement/split-second timing.

Instead, he said, "You know, you have a kind of standard face."

Holly took a step back, but amazingly didn't take offense. "It goes with my transmission," she said in a friendly low voice.

Neil was running his finger along the cracked weather stripping of the open door. "No, oh, well, I mean, some faces confuse you."

And she, in one motion, smooth and swift—as, say, shifting into third gear—kissed him. A kiss with gentleness and passion fruit–flavored lipstick, and yes, he wasn't just kidding himself—passion itself.

"Your face is pretty standard, too," she said.

Thus began the dizzy stage of their relationship where all common ground proved they were meant for each other. Their phone numbers were only two digits apart. Their middle names began with an *L*. But then Holly took Neil hiking on Squaw Peak and hinted of his meeting her family. They sat on a U-Haul sized boulder and looked down on the shaggy green palms and blue squares of swimming pool. He hiccuped when she mentioned her family.

"Tell me about your family," she said then.

"My mother died in a fire six months ago." Neil told how her water heater had malfunctioned. He remembered the ponytailed fire chief tapping his clipboard rhythmically against his shiny badge and how he had listened to the tapping, hoping that it might signal additional information, something to make his mother's death not true or at least less painful. Neil said, "My mother believed you could prevent a disaster by worrying about it. She spent her life issuing warnings: Don't eat after midnight; don't bathe during a thunderstorm; don't watch TV in the dark. She was always worrying about dying. And then she died."

Holly slipped her hand into his. The thrill of it caused something musical to happen along his spine. He thought he should tell her more about how his mother's death had changed everything, as the first gunshot turns a battle scene into a battle. It had been one thing for his mother to be scared of dying and quite an impossible, bewildering other thing for her actually to be dead. But Holly's hand felt so nice, weightless yet reassuring. It comforted him. He looked toward the America West Arena and the old Westward Ho Hotel and thought how if he weren't so scared of heights this would be a great view.

Holly said, "I'm sorry about your mom. My mother is a nut. She bangs on the table with a shoe. She threatens to run us through the Cuisinart, a body part at a time. But I can't even think of her being gone. When she dies, I know after I get over the relief of not having to listen to her, I'll be sorry that I can't."

Neil sighed. "That's exactly what I mean." He thought how his mother's death made everything seem sadder. As his sister Robin had said when she cried over some burned chicken and dumplings, "It starts out about a ruined dinner or a stained handbag, and it ends up about Mamma." Neil rested his elbow on the warm rock, feeling relaxed—happy and sad both. So comfortable that he kissed Holly, rather spontaneously, without stopping to worry about noses or teeth.

This was a serious relationship. But then everything was serious for the Pruitts: cutter bees in the tomato plants, homemade signs telling about lost Alaskan huskies. And now death and love both, almost simultaneously.

The day after the hike Holly invited Neil to lunch with her family. "They want to meet you," she said, flipping over a red checker piece. "King me."

"Your whole family?" he said, fumbling with the crowning part.

"Just my parents and brothers. I've talked so much about you."

He said, "I see," rubbing the embossed crown with his thumb, realizing what you hope and what you fear can be exactly the same thing.

But what had she said about him? He thought of her explaining with trembling excitement that he was—was what? Dependable? Contentious? No, no, maybe something else. Maybe it was like Lois Lane glimpsing something promising in Clark Kent. Confused, intrigued. "Clark, I was wondering what you looked like without your glasses." Guessing.

"Sure, lunch," he said with purposeful nonchalance. "It's just a meal."

On the day of the lunch Neil's head ached so badly he took an overdose of Anacin. It caused a ringing in his ears that wavered like a bad frequency, cutting in and out—loud when he and Holly passed the elderly golfers at Encanto Park and quieter when their car stalled behind the bus with the huge pictures of the Channel 12 News Team. But his headache had improved, though he'd lost some language. Words like *lawn* were being warped to *lawnd. Freeway* had disappeared entirely.

Holly said, "Are you nervous?"

Ordering food at a restaurant made Neil nervous, or placing a collect call, test-driving a car. "No," he said, "not really."

When he'd told Kenneth he was meeting Holly's family, Kenneth had tucked in his shirt. He'd asked how many were in the family, as if Neil would be expected to arm wrestle each one.

"She has two brothers," Neil said, "and her parents."

Kenneth winced. Neil had been counting on more reassurance. "That's not so many people," Kenneth finally said. He was putting up a towel rack, placing it way too high, as if it were for chin-ups.

"It's four," Neil said. He'd like to see Kenneth take on a woman's family. When was the last time Kenneth even had a date?

Kenneth said, "I think women like to see how you'll fit in with the family, check out the interpersonal dynamics." He'd been talking like that since his promotion to the water conservation board.

"Hm," Neil said, turning on the cold water tap, turning it off, trying not to take it too much to heart. Yet.

"Hand me that screwdriver, will you, Neil? My advice? Be as charming as you can possibly be."

Neil slapped the tool into Kenneth's hand. Kenneth nodded, worked the screwdriver, biting on his tongue. Neil turned on the water, divided the stream with his finger. Their mother had called Kenneth the bravest Pruitt, but Neil thought he would show Kenneth real courage, the kind you only get from being in love.

"Something big might come of this," Neil said, liking the way he said it, the boastful swagger in his voice.

But all Kenneth said was "Yeah, let us know. Hey, Neil, do you mind turning off that water? It's kind of my job, you know?"

When they got to the Svensons' house it reminded Neil of gangsters. It had awnings and shutters, as if it had something to hide. The tinkling of Holly's mother's bracelets tricked his hearing. Her father had on a Perry Como sweater. Her brothers, men who looked like Vikings, had plates overfull with strange food: fruit in odd mutations, breads with black seeds like insects, or worse.

Mr. Svenson told Neil what he had paid for the sculpture in the front hall—told Neil, *after* he'd asked Neil to guess.

"Guess?" Neil said.

"Oh, Dad!" Holly said. Neil was thinking *what next?*—flipping through possible disasters like index cards, hoping to find the right wrong thing that would happen before it happened, so by thinking about it they could miss it. But then Mrs. Svenson decided to nail Mr. Svenson with one of the altered fruits, and it became, as it had with his mother's water heater, too late.

"Hell's bells," Mr. Svenson said, surprisingly levelheaded, surprisingly not surprised, checking for blood, but licking fruit juice off his fingers instead.

"Serves you right," Mrs. Svenson said, picking up a knife, trying to balance it on her arm.

"Rambo," a brother yelled.

A dog of mixed heritage, some part dalmatian, part collie, stood in the doorway. At the sound of its name, it backed out of the room.

"He does tricks," Holly said.

"Oh?" Neil said.

Mrs. Svenson said, "He turns on the dishwasher, turns off the alarm clock."

"Neil," Holly said, "I've got to show you something." She took his hand and led him through the double French doors, past the modern sculpture shaped like an immense dish detergent bottle. Somewhere a grandfather clock bonged like a sentencing, and Holly and Neil entered a small bedroom at the back of the house.

The room had ballerina wallpaper. The dancers balanced, leapt, and curtsied, and all looked just the same. A yellow chenille bedspread with indentations like the tracks of a rake covered a maple bed. Holly's old bedroom. There was passivity in a monkey sock-doll, quietude in maroon volumes of *The Book of Knowledge.* An old calendar hung on the wall, dates circled with frail pencil lines.

Holly flopped on the bed, patted a spot for Neil beside her. "You were dying at lunch, weren't you?"

"No. They are, your family is—"

"Not standard."

"No, not so standard," he said, and he breathed in the luxurious peace and buried his fingertips in the chenille's furrows.

The bed faced a window, looked out on an orange grove where

the trees were trimmed like open umbrellas and all the trunks were painted white.

"They are careless people," Holly said. "They leave behind muddy footprints and dirty dishes, and then are terribly upset by other people's muddy footprints and dirty dishes." She touched her collar with a short settling stroke, and Neil saw fingers endearingly hangnailed. "They wreck cars. They turn over furniture. They throw whatever's in their hands: books—I've seen a biography of Samuel Johnson knock six lit candles out of a candelabra. The portable television once landed in some borscht. Eggs, a whole omelet, dropped on the floor, to prove—to *prove*—that they were *not* hard-boiled. It's impossible." She bunched the pillow under her head. A habit, he saw, a comfort from the days when she lived in this wild house.

"My parents are proud of their passion. Love is loud, they say. I've disappointed them because I'm not loud, and I don't like loud. But I used to try. I'd bring home friends to show them that even though I was predictable I could make friends who were not. But—" She pulled on a hangnail. Neil held his breath, waiting for it to bleed, hoping it wouldn't. "It was like eating lunch sitting on explosives. Anxious and possibly very loud." She paused. "You know, I don't really have anything to show you. I was just trying to get you away from them." She pointed to a chipped dresser. "I could show you my high-jump medals or my petrified wood from the Petrified Forest."

"What's this?" Neil said, pointing to a stack of papers on the nightstand.

"Spelling tests," Holly said shyly. "I'd review them before I went to bed. One of those weird kid self-improvement kicks. I still can't spell."

"I did it with the capitals of states. Somehow I pictured myself working on a secret military assignment, and the mission would depend on someone knowing the capital of Delaware." Actually, he'd been good at memorizing. Remembering that suddenly made him content. Now the buzz in his ears was comfortable, more like a purr. He noticed a smudged birthmark on Holly's neck—shaped, in fact, like an Eastern Seaboard state—and he thought how those imperfections of loved ones become precious and even handsome. He touched Holly's neck, the smooth shape of the flaw.

"Pruitt!" Mr. Svenson barked from the doorway. Holly and Neil jumped up. "Ready for a tour of the homestead?"

Mrs. Svenson led her husband, Neil, and Holly through the living room with its matching pink plaid chairs big enough for giants, past the chess table with its pieces like medieval weaponry, pausing once to shove a rock from the Berlin Wall at Neil and a photograph of a naked three-year-old Holly sitting on some railroad tracks. "Come, come," Mrs. Svenson said in an Alice-in-Wonderland hurry. Neil wanted to sit down, to think about things: that food, the spelling tests, a toddler on railroad tracks?

They came to the swimming pool. A stone sea serpent spat water into the shallow end. The humps of its back arched above a Mexican bird of paradise. Rambo lapped water and jumped when Holly's brother yelled his name. So far, Neil liked the dog best.

"Holly, telephone," the brother yelled again from the door.

Neil watched her go. Mrs. Svenson pulled some sunglasses from a pocket in her billowy pastel skirt. Tiny circles of sun reflected in each tiny circle of lens when she turned a satisfied smile to Neil. "Neil, dear. Aren't we glad you came today?"

Neil grinned. What was he supposed to say?

Mrs. Svenson said, "Holly has talked about you," then to Mr. Svenson, "hasn't she, darling?"

Mr. Svenson was straightening the bills in his money clip. "Hm?" he said.

"Of course she has. And we've been looking forward to meeting you, someone so—so—stable." So *that's* what Holly said about him. Mrs. Svenson whipped off her sunglasses and began to chew on an ear piece. "Holly's dated some real weirdos." She pointed the sunglasses at Neil, gestured up and down with them in appraisal, slowing to a dissatisfied belt-level stop. "Remember that race car driver? Wasn't he a demolition derby expert or something? And the guy whose life's ambition was to jump off Hoover Dam with a bungee cord. Wouldn't that kill you, Ed? If you did that?"

Mr. Svenson said, "The Christian Scientist was ordinary enough, too, though."

"But that sneezing and sniffling! And she dropped him flat, didn't she?" Mrs. Svenson put her glasses back on, looking pleased, as if the dropping had been suggested by her.

Dropped the ordinary guy, Neil thought, not missing the connection.

"So, tell us about the Pruitts," Mrs. Svenson said.

Neil thought of his family, orderly as the alphabet, befuddled by clock radios and answering machines. Kenneth gulped Excedrin and arranged his pencils by length. Robin sometimes vacuumed her garage.

Neil said, "My brother Kenneth works for the water department. My sister Robin just got married."

"And you've lost both your parents?" Mrs. Svenson said.

Her word choice confused him, because the Pruitts were, in fact, often lost, setting out for destinations with maps and extra water, often a snack.

"Didn't Holly tell me that your mother died recently?" Mrs. Svenson said.

They looked at him. Soberly, but with somewhat ghoulish expectations. Suddenly he doubted Holly's affection for him. Was it even possible, coming from this family? Was she proving something to her parents by having him as a boyfriend? A different something than she'd been proving with the others?

"How did she die?" They said it together.

How he longed to be interesting! He stood up taller. He announced, "She was killed."

"Wow," they gasped. "That's awful!"

Neil rubbed his forehead where it hurt the most, just over his eyes. He saw the trap he'd made for himself, realizing how ridiculous her death would sound to people who teased disaster with a red flag; laughed at it; flirted with it, sweet heaven, *dated* it. His mother had died in bed, killed by a household appliance—albeit a major one.

"Goodness," they said, with another flash of bloodthirsty satisfaction. "How was she killed?"

They had him.

"A hot water heater." He saw disappointment slip from their eyes, coming to rest at the corners of their mouths.

"Boom," he said weakly, fists opening and distance expanding between his hands, like a joke or a cartoon.

The Pruitts often said the wrong thing, often made it worse. Now Neil was ready to say something even stupider, except he was silenced by his fear of losing Holly, as well as a suffocating grief for his mother. How he missed and suddenly admired her! A woman who cooked dependably with cheese that was orange and bread that was white.

Holly's parents stared at him, Mrs. Svenson even took her sunglasses back off.

"Neil and I'll clean up," Holly said, returning. She clapped her hands once in front and once behind her, like a young girl going out to recess, innocently unaware.

In the kitchen, Neil scraped the dishes. Carefully, purposefully wiping off the food, he tried to do something right, hoping in some way to make himself worthy.

Holly said, "My mom is *proud* of not owning a cookbook. I don't think she ever notices how the food actually tastes." She flipped on the garbage disposal. "The boys want to get some kind of game together. Blackjack, I believe. They don't think I know they gamble. You don't gamble, do you?"

"No." Wasn't living risky enough?

"Anyway, I won't let them drag you in. How's your head?"

"Better." It was what he always said.

"My mother has a theory that the farther north your ancestors come from, the better stock you are; the more interesting. I made up a country for your people. This morning I saw her checking for it on the globe." Holding butter shaped like a cow udder, she opened the refrigerator, but it was already bulging with appallingly imaginative food. "Does she really think that the people in North Dakota are more worthwhile than the people in South Dakota? Hell's bells. Say," she said, over her shoulder, "does anyone know the capitals of North and South Dakota?"

"Bismarck and Pierre," he said, wishing he could make it sound romantic or adventuresome. But she smiled as brightly as if it had been. And he wanted to make something of it; hint that she'd probably never dated a man with such extraordinary geographic skills.

A brother stuck his head in the door. "Neil, gin rummy? Hearts? Blackjack?"

The other brother came in. He flexed various muscles, called the roll. "Deltoid." His shoulder responded. "Pectoralis major," he said to his chest. "Trapezius," he said, not to any muscle, it seemed, but menacingly to Neil.

"Dessert?" Mrs. Svenson entered the room in changed clothes, a blue blouse with thunderbirds and zigzags. "Who wants Flan Svenson?"

After dessert some people came over, drifted in, casual as a chaise lounge. First was a burly man, Al Romney, who kept talking about his traffic ticket for going through a parking lot instead of sitting "like a damn fool" waiting for a red light to change. His wife appeared skeptical in wire-rimmed glasses. Next came the Folleys, a couple as sturdy as Whirlpool washers. Then the Mackenzie brothers in Stanford T-shirts, who looked like dark-haired Svenson brothers.

Neil passed the coffee Mrs. Svenson had handed him, forgot the word for it, just once. Fighting Chinese porcelain frogs flanked the fireplace. On the piano, a stern blue and white vase sprouted tropical flowers, fake but luxuriant as a rain forest. Neil felt a tug on his pants leg, and a girl with a Bugs Bunny Band-Aid across her skimpy chin said, "Are you going to eat your cherry?"

The ringing in his ears had a vibration, a small bumblebee motion causing a pinch of claustrophobia. The room was filling up, like air into an already overfull balloon.

A man fussing with his pearly cowboy buttons said, "I hear y'all are cooking up a game."

A brother had Neil by the shoulder, had taken him from Holly.

"I'm coming," Holly called to him, holding up a finger.

But Al Romney was yelling at her, "Can you imagine getting a ticket for driving past Smitty's?"

The brother led Neil into a large room with other men and shelves of trophies, shiny figures frozen in intimidating contortions. Nearby, a suit of armor stood guard.

"What do you say, Neil?" A brother wiped his mouth on the back of his hand.

The other brother said, "It's easy. Two cards, tell the dealer to hit you."

"Hit me?"

"You got it." He scratched his chest. "If you've got to be a bear, be a grizzly."

From the living room Neil heard a crash and Mrs. Svenson's scream, "You take that, you idiot. I won't listen to that."

"Mother!" Holly wailed. She wouldn't be coming soon.

Panic spread like a spilled liquid inside Neil's chest, seeping into agitated crevices.

"Bathroom," he announced.

"Twenty-one," someone said. "Tell my mamma I'm going to be rich."

"Has the dealer come?"

Neil slipped out the door. As he hurried by one of the rooms, he heard a frantic whisper, "An egg shape is an ellipse." There were quick footsteps behind him. He ducked into Holly's room, opened another door, stepped in, closed it. A closet. Dark. Dark as the whale to Jonah. A two-man closet, at most. But relief welled inside him. He was safe.

What felt like cheerleading pom-poms made a dry, muted *chh* when he pushed them aside to slide down. The hem of some garment draped on his shoulder. A door slammed. The dog barked. And at last, his head didn't hurt anymore.

Bitterly, he pictured Kenneth at home heating up some Heinz beans and wienies and some peas, fresh from the Green Giant can. There was a whimpering at the closet door, a scratching. What now? What *now?* An animal whine. When Neil opened the door a crack, Rambo squeezed in. The hangers skidded on the rod as Rambo's tail wagged into the clothes. Neil felt the sympathy of the dog's dry tongue on his face.

Rambo must have yawned, for suddenly Neil smelled fecund dog breath. "You see," Neil began, "I broke my leg skiing the first time I went. My nose was broken by a tennis ball, and I was just watching. It's hard to be courageous when there's so little reward for it."

Water was running somewhere. The telephone rang once.

What am I doing? Neil thought. How will I get out? He felt as stuck as if all the Svensons had watched him go in. He imagined himself emerging blinking into the light, his hair rumpled as an unmade bed. Years later. Rip Van Pruitt. Questions would be asked.

He waited, moved his legs, trying to stir their prickly bloodlessness. He touched something plastic by his foot, rubbed knobby protrusions, until he realized they were a Barbie doll's breasts.

His mother had organized her family's fears, updated them like news bulletins. They were the first on their block to be concerned about lead in pottery. At the initial reported outbreak of *E. coli* contamination, they had given up beef. *Informed* worriers. But what had it helped?

He heard music, the Rascals screeching "Mustang Sally." What in the world? He leaned his head against the dog. Was it rescue he longed for? Kenneth and Robin coming to save him? Scattered applause. Someone yelled, "Ooo, shake it!"

Maybe he would get bored enough to leave. Or hungry. Sooner or later something would get him out. But what would it matter? By then the damage would have been done. He was sitting in a closet. In his girlfriend's closet. His girlfriend who was accustomed to bungee cord–jumper boyfriends. A different kind of strange than his. Maybe her feelings for him were just a phase she was going through. Or maybe he was a message to her parents—to scare them. Maybe he was her revenge.

Then in the dark, way overdue, he recalled that Lois Lane had no interest at all in Clark Kent. She had eyes only for Superman. The Man of Steel, who could fly her past prop-driven airplanes, and after the planet Earth had spun dizzyingly beneath them, cradle her tenderly to her balcony door. And anyway, under Clark Kent's button-down shirt there was always the red, yellow, and blue bulge of a Superman uniform, while under Neil's shirt was only the scrawny chest of a quiet man in love. What was love worth from a man who couldn't even look over the edge of Hoover Dam, never mind the jumping?

He heard footsteps in the bedroom, saw movement in the line of light under the closet door. "Rambo," Holly called. "Here, Rambo."

The dog got to his feet, wagged his tail into the clothes. Neil grabbed him to keep him still. It was silent out in the bedroom, as Neil held his breath.

Holly spoke, her voice ordinary and informational. "There's some Anacin in the bathroom if you need it." Neil heard her leave, the closing click of the outside door.

That was it, he knew, all he would get. Now. He stood, shook down his pants, stepped out into the light. Rambo stretched his own hairy legs.

"You don't really do tricks, do you?" he said to the dog.

Rambo walked to the door, nosed on the light.

Neil found everyone in the living room: the neighbors, the Svensons, the gamblers. The food from lunch had been put back on the dining room table, the salad with pasta shaped like donkeys and elephants, the purple and yellow olives, the huge pickles, warty as witches. The group stomped and wiggled. Seizures, trances, swooning: a dance. They had found a new diversion, changed directions, quick as a school of fish.

Holly walked to him through the middle of the crowd. She had restyled her hair, combed it up off her neck. He was struck by the beauty of her Connecticut-shaped birthmark. He moved toward her, offering what he could: a standard face, Clark Kent without a Superman backup.

"I found the dog," Neil said.

"I see you did." She extended her arm to him, bent gracefully at the elbow, a beckoning as comforting as a guardrail, reassuring as a red wagon.

Relieved, he stepped toward her, but then paused with one last fear.

He said, "I can't dance."

Her smile. "Yes, I know."

Survival Rates

For the first time in two days, Wilson thinks Janice may have run out of questions. Hopes it. He watches her put a bag of groceries on the table. She steadies and situates it like a new lamp, stands back as if she's checking how it looks against the pine cupboards and the Mexican tile floor.

"Any more in the car?" Wilson says.

"What?"

"Can I help?" He pushes aside the door's curtain, sees the dusty Toyota's trunk is closed. Above the car clouds are gathering over the dark green pines of the Mogollon Rim.

Janice says, "So the radioactive iodine is supposed to kill the rest of the thyroid, even the part that's not malignant?"

"Yeah, the cells suck it up." Wilson puts the Ragu in the cupboard, the bread and butter pickles in the refrigerator.

Since yesterday, when the doctor confirmed his thyroid cancer, Janice and Wilson have talked and talked about it. It reminds him of working on road construction, driving a steel-wheeled vibrating roller over a lift of asphalt, a numbing back and forth that makes no apparent difference.

Janice holds a cantaloupe in both palms, seems to be communing with it.

Dr. Rodgers, insisting that cancers have personalities, has told them thyroid cancer lacks any real oncological ambition. He's called it shiftless, an embarrassment to the whole cancer community. Colo-rectal, he said, wants it kicked out entirely.

"I-131, the magic bullet," Wilson says now.

Janice's smile is as undirected as a leaf falling. The Persian cat, Theodora, feigning invisibility to mask her humiliation, nibbles at her food. She seems to understand that the groomer's "lion cut" makes her look like a creature from Dr. Seuss.

Janice and Wilson sit on the redwood deck of their small cabin in Kohl's Ranch, drinking Orange Royale tea flavored with sage honey. Over the Rim, the sky is the charcoal color of a business suit. As the storm develops, it will slip over the cliffs, its color more transparent as it comes, as if it's trying to sneak up on them. A bad storm can cut off the power to their place, may even wash out the red dirt road. Wilson wouldn't mind that. They could light those fat candles that smell like vanilla and almond and wrap themselves in his grandmother's drunkard's-progress quilt, abandon themselves to the theatrics of nature: the woeful ponderosa pines, the thunder vengeful as the Old Testament. But storms make Janice tense; she dislikes weather.

A rabbit hops from a clump of Indian Paintbrush to a spot just under Wilson's old white pickup truck. It sniffs the air from behind a split-rim Firestone.

Wilson talks about his landscaping firm. "Judy and Ed were in today ordering ten flats of petunias. They'd heard some joker on the radio say javelina don't eat them."

"They sure ate up the pansies," Janice says.

"Pig salad."

"I hate javelina," Janice says, rubbing the backs of her arms, as if she's cold. "I've heard their fur stands up all over just before they charge you. Does it?"

"I've never seen one actually charge. Anyway, I think they're pretty blind." Wilson doesn't know if this is so, but he wants to extend this pleasant conversation, pleasant because it's not about cancer and also because he can be reassuring about something as unlikely as a wild pig attack. Husbands should be comforting, he thinks, knowledgeable too, if possible.

"They eat cactus," he says. "Prickly pear, even the spines. Jerry said he saw a bunch of them the other night when he was riding. Just their eyeshine. He said he wasn't sure who was more spooked, him or the horse." Jerry is his partner at Pinetop Landscape and Nursery—when it's not rodeo season. They have an ongoing debate about the morality of deer hunting, Wilson taking the passivist side. They also share a delight in porno movie titles. It was Jerry who recognized what Wilson calls "Horatio Alger pornography." "Plucky," Jerry had said, "that's all you can call those girls." Janice had said, "There are probably other things, too."

"Javelina are tough pigs," Janice says. She picks up her *Teaching Adds Up* mug. "So, how remote is the possibility of severing the vocal cord nerve during surgery?" She bites her lip, *assaults* it. She has cancer questions, is helpless to stop them.

Wilson touches his throat. "Oh," he says, "remote, *re-mote.* Hey, let's play Scrabble. I feel lucky and wordy."

"Verbose," Janice says, mechanically.

"Great Scrabble word," Wilson says.

/ / /

In the morning Janice reads their horoscopes in the *Mogollon Advisor.* Hers says she should test international waters. She pauses thoughtfully, as if high school math teachers have international waters. Wilson's forecast warns him to beware of complicating emotions generated by friends from the past.

When they were first married, two years ago, he was charmed by her reading horoscopes. Out of character, he thought, for a mathematician. Lately he's decided Janice's horoscope interest isn't out of character, just the extreme of her need to understand, veering in this case toward the superstitious. She also reads instruction booklets and nutritional information, can report on obscure functions of electrical appliances. "Dazzling," he said when she told him about the microwave beverage feature. She said, "Ah, it's nothing," and smacked him on the arm.

Theodora darts from the windowsill to a spot under Janice's chair. She is not a lap cat, but will tolerate a chuck under the chin.

"Here, kitty, kitty," he calls to her, just to prove to himself how she won't come.

Janice smooths the creases in the newspaper, reads aloud, "The Kohl's Ranch annual craft fair will attract vendors from all over the region. There will be homemade goodies and art."

"I like my art homemade," Wilson says.

Janice tells him that Charlene, one of the other teachers at her school, is selling T-shirts, signs, plaques.

"*God bless this house?*" Wilson says.

She says, "Stuff like *Miracles happen* and *Kiss the cook.*"

"Important stuff. We'd better go."

"To the craft fair? My school kids would call it cheesy."

Wilson says, "Cheesy is in the eye of the beholder." He sees she is reluctant to go, would feel safer at home with the doors closed. "It'll be fun," he says.

/ / /

The fair sprawls along Highway 87, the road that goes to the Rim. Booths are set up around some bristlecone spruce and quaking aspen. Wilson parks in the free-for-all of a small dirt parking lot near where the Verde River runs along the highway, changing the air, cooling and stirring it.

There is a bewildering variety of fair goods, but they are still curiously all the same, as if they've been made by a communal mind. Wilson looks for clues he may have missed about society. Holidays, apparently, need decoration: Christmas angels with closed eyes and ceramic jack-o'-lanterns with boxy teeth. Bunnies and bears are made out of wood, yarn, even stone. On a shelf, a small herd of gray felt javelina grins good-naturedly, their usually muscular shoulders plump instead with fiberfill.

"Let's buy something," he says. "Look at that bed tray." It is wooden with compartments, a vase for a rose.

Janice looks stricken. What has he said? Bed tray? Sick? All conversation leads to cancer, he sees now.

She says, "Let's just get one of the homemade goodies."

They are looking at the Rice Krispies treats and Sandy's Tastie Pops when Janice says, "There's Charlene. I'd better say hello."

Charlene is a tall, serene woman. Janice has said the kids like her but don't respect her. She's wearing a T-shirt with *Life is noth-*

ing without garlic on it. A pillow on her counter reads, *My other pillow is a goose down.* Several chef's aprons are clothespinned to a line. They are cross-stitched with *I'm not aging, I'm marinating.* Charlene smiles. There's a friendly gap in her teeth.

"I didn't expect to see *you* here," she says to Janice.

As Wilson watches Janice hook her dark hair behind her ear, he realizes there are craft-fair types. Janice is not one.

Janice says, "Who could stay away?" The leaves on the aspen tree by Charlene's booth flutter, flashing their silvery undersides.

Wilson picks up a key chain shaped like a golf ball: *I only play golf on days that end in Y.* He says to Charlene, "Do you make up all of these?"

"Just some," she says.

"Which ones?" Wilson says. "Which are your best-sellers? Which are your favorites?" Sheepishly, he realizes *he* is the craft-fair type.

Janice says, "Wilson." She thinks his questions too personal. He asks people if they've found new jobs or if they've patched it up with their wives. He likes to give encouragement and support. "There are angels among us," he remembers his mother saying about people who were kind to them when his father died too young.

"My favorite?" Charlene says. She holds up a T-shirt that says, *All I need to know about life I learned from my cat.*

"Yes." He's speaking too loudly. "I'll take it."

/ / /

After surgery, Wilson hears a voice from a dark distance calling his name. It is firm, insistent, asking him to speak. "Just say *eee.*"

He says, "*Eee*," opens his eyes to a smiling Dr. Rodgers and the anesthesiologist.

"Vocal cord nerve intact," Dr. Rodgers says. A blue-capped woman writes it down.

There's a tightness across Wilson's neck.

/ / /

After he gets home he must keep his neck dry. Janice washes his hair. He looks in the mirror, says that's better, though she's combed it in that brushed-back way women comb their own hair.

Jerry brings over a pony pack of begonias to wish him a speedy recovery. "Your neck's swollen," he says. "Don't go and button your top button." He tells Janice all the customers want Wilson back at the shop because he'll talk to them about whether a cottonwood will get too big near their house trailers and about what kind of flowers go with junipers. He aims a finger gun at his temple, shakes his head.

When Janice goes to get them some coffee, Jerry fakes a leer. "*Tits a Wonderful Life*," he says.

"I heard that," Janice calls from the kitchen.

Wilson yells, "Heard what?" but says in a stage whisper, "*A Clockwork Orgy*."

Janice brings in a tray, says, "It's the literary illusions that make them so classy."

Jerry shows Wilson some plans for a house by the Verde River, tells him about the waterfall on the property, pauses to ask one of the crazy but earnest questions Jerry is known for: "Janice, is there a formula for figuring how much water goes over a waterfall?"

"Probably," Janice says, "but it's physics, not math."

Jerry says, "They want to divert water for a pond."

"*On Golden Blond*," Wilson says and watches amazed as Theodora jumps into Jerry's lap.

"What have you done to this cat?" Jerry says.

/ / /

The next day Janice starts asking questions during "Twilight Zone." She wants to know why and how the cancer started. Wilson is in a La-Z-Boy eating a peanut butter and jam sandwich. Between his elevated feet, beneficent bulbous-headed space creatures are teaching the earthlings how to grow more food.

"Do you think you were exposed to something?" Janice says. "High-voltage electrical lines? Defoliants?" She makes a grocery list of carcinogens. The government official on the show tries to decipher the language in the aliens' book, *To Serve Man*.

"Pesticides?"

Wilson says, "No. I mean, maybe."

Fifteen minutes later Janice says, "Do you think it was from the way we eat? Your dad died of heart disease, didn't he? Has anyone else had cancer?"

"This is a good part," he says, motioning to the TV and licking a smudge of peanut butter off his thumb. "They've been fattening the humans up." He grins.

But Janice is reading. "I wish we could know." She speaks into the pages of the pamphlet from the doctor, "Thyroid Cancer: It Can Be Cured."

"Let's get out," Wilson says, turning off the TV.

They walk on a path soft with dust. He tells about the letter he got from his sister Lily, an energetic and guilty worrier, telling how in the confessional her new priest had told her to go buy herself a root beer float.

"Penance?" Janice says.

When Wilson nods, she says, "One smart priest."

He tells her his truck is running rough. He's going to get some Gum-Out before he takes it to the repair shop. He says Jerry's been trying to sell those fifteen olive trees he mistakenly ordered by telling customers they haven't lived until they've had fresh olives on their pizza.

"What's going on in school?" he says. "Are the kids getting lost yet in trig?"

"We bought TI-85s for that class," she says.

"They'll probably just play computer games on them."

"I don't want to know," she says.

He tells her their outing is a nature walk. Tree frogs are tenacious. Skunks are convivial. He shows her his favorite shrub, the manzanita, a handsome plant indigenous to the area, with gnarled maroon branches that bleed into red-veined leaves. It cannot be cultivated or transplanted; dies when it is moved. The path ends in a dried-up creek. Its cracked-mud bed is littered with jumbled boulders and tree skeletons. A giant's refuse.

Janice kicks a stone. "What kind of sin do you think you'd have to commit to get a hot fudge sundae?" she says.

/ / /

One evening after the stitches are out, Wilson opens the front door to a student of Janice's, a girl named Niki. She has come with her boyfriend, a short kid with a quarterback name. The boy wears a ridiculous Indiana Jones hat. Niki herself is chirpy optimism. Janice has told him she quotes Goethe, calling him "Go-thee": "Boldness has genius and magic in it."

Niki hands Wilson a plate of sugar cookies. He recognizes a saguaro, an apple, a flower. "Kind of a landscaping theme," Niki says, with a giggle that makes Wilson think, *schoolgirl*.

Janice says, "That's so nice of you. Hi, Joe. Sit down."

They continue to stand. Niki says to Wilson, "How are you doing there?" A teenager speaking to an adult, she doesn't call him by name, but she glances at his neck.

"Not bad," he says. "I have a manly scar."

Janice clucks her tongue, rolls her eyes, as if he's showing off, laying rubber, peeling out.

Wilson says, "Like a slashed throat. A wound from the war." He lifts his head patriotically.

"*The* war." Janice is mock-solemn.

"Or," he says, "I'm going to tell people a woman did it to me. A very angry woman." He furrows his brow, a world-weary look, takes a drag on an imaginary cigarette. "A Spanish prostitute." He flicks the cigarette away.

Janice says, "For heaven's sake." She closes her eyes tightly, as if she's trying to remember where she put something, but then she begins to laugh, with such energy it seems aerobic. Wilson thinks she married him because he made her laugh, though it always seems to surprise her, catch her off guard, like a whale surfacing from a great depth—unlike her response to calamity, which she accepts like a letter she's been expecting.

She wipes her eyes on her sleeve. "What am I going to do with you?" she says, but he can see the question is partly serious.

Niki tells them she sent in her scholarship application for U.S.C. She says her father is bragging down at the Minit-Lube just that she applied. As they leave, she hands Janice a homework paper. "Sorry there's pizza grease," she says. "And it's late."

Janice takes it, says, "Hm, well."

/ / /

Leaving for the hospital, Janice says, "He said you'd have to stay three days?"

"If I'm lucky, only two."

"Isn't anaplastic the rare kind that's usually fatal?"

"I don't have that," Wilson says, patiently. He's begun to feel like he's being drilled for a test, primed to give correct cancer answers.

Janice says, "It's more common in women."

"Yes," he says. "I'm not that either. Maybe it's something to mention to Lily, especially if it seems to run in families." He wonders when he started giving in to this urge to be sarcastic. He would have guessed sarcastic was something people had quit being. He checks the gas gauge and is irritated to find it low. He's hungry from the low-iodine diet he's been on. Why can't she let it alone? "The ten-year survival rate is in the upper ninetieth percentile," he adds by way of apology and reassurance. He knows the survival rate because she told him, one of many, many things she told him.

Janice pauses in adjusting the visor against the morning sun. "Still," she says. Another irritation, her insistence that things might be worse than they really are.

The truck stirs some dust. Janice cranks the window knob up. On the edge of their property they pass the boulders. In size and shape they resemble three Volkswagens, slightly irregular and red. They are stacked on top of each other like a fraternity prank. The bottom one is the roundest, making the formation appear precarious.

Janice says, "I wish you'd get your Cat from work and knock

those over, so they won't fall on their own and do some real damage."

"They've been here since the Ice Age."

"What if they fall when the mailman's driving below them or if they slip in a storm and block the road? We can't just sit around waiting for it to happen."

She looks like a mistress on TV whose lover won't leave his wife. Annoyed. Disappointed. Distressed. This is Janice trying to meet disaster head-on rather than sitting around wondering when or whether it will happen—the mentality of that woodsman who cut off his leg when it was trapped under a tree. Wilson suddenly can see Janice doing that. A superhuman courage born of superhuman fear and impatience. Amazing and kind of scary.

Janice looks out the window. "I don't think it'll make you that sick," she says, returning to the real issue. "Thirsty is all, a little nausea."

He whistles, thinking instead about the owl he heard last night, probably a Great Gray, that the *who* was exactly that sound, an owl sounding like an owl imitation.

"At least whistle a tune," Janice says. "You sound like some bird."

/ / /

A big nurse, rugged as a plow, brings the radioactive iodine in a wheelchair. It's in a box draped with a lead blanket. She uses tongs to get the capsules out, two white ones, too big for humans. After he's swallowed them, she waves a Geiger counter over his stomach, a beefy fairy godmother.

"Flush the toilet three times," she says, backing out the wheelchair.

They leave his lunch tray by the door. He reads Tom Clancy with plastic gloves so as not to contaminate the book. In the afternoon he counts off the hours on the classroom-sized clock, then he counts off the minutes until he can count off the hours.

Janice doesn't come until after dinner.

"Hey there," he calls, happy to see her.

She stands next to a radioactive warning sign behind the red vinyl tape line on the floor, clutching a bouquet of sunflowers and some magazines. She's wearing her glasses. Wilson thinks they make her look determined. She turns to watch an orderly push a laundry cart past.

"How are you?" she says.

"I can change the TV channel without the remote control. I can probably start cars in the parking lot."

"Don't say that." She holds her hand up like a traffic cop.

Wilson says, "I'll be home soon. The Geiger counter pulse is at thirty. I've been drinking a lot of water."

Janice looks at the carpet, digs at the tape with her toe.

"My neck only hurts a little." The questions haven't been asked, and his answers feel too small. He says, "Did the truck drive OK?"

"Yeah."

"Did Jerry pick up payroll?"

"Sure. There's a get-well card from him."

"Does Theodora miss me?"

Not even a smile.

Something in her seems to have snapped shut. The treatment has left a bad taste in his mouth. He peels the paper on cherry Lifesavers and starts to offer her one, forgetting about having touched it. He thinks of King Midas.

"I've got cabin fever," he says. "No one here gets near me or anything I've touched. It's weird." But it's more than that; it's lonely, too.

"Radioactive," Janice says.

Radioactive like the fifties or a Hollywood movie. Meryl Streep —they scrubbed her with stiff brushes in a shower.

"Have you talked to Dr. Rodgers?" Janice asks.

"No."

"Radioactive," she says again, under her breath, but with disgust, as if they—someone—has subjected Wilson to something humiliating. "You don't ask enough questions. You don't seem to even really want to know. I've got to go."

She shoves the flowers and magazines over to his side of the tape.

"Wait," he says, but it's after she's left.

He reties the drawstring on the hospital scrubs he's wearing. He would like to approach his illness cautiously, while Janice would yank it up by its hair to look it in the face. Fear makes her aggressive, he knows.

Once they came home to an intruder in the cabin, a boy holding one of the striped pillowcases—itself stolen from under their bedspread—bulging with their belongings. Wilson's only foggy conviction was he must take Janice and leave immediately and hope the guy might forgive their intrusion. But Janice had actually walked *toward* the boy. "What are you doing here?" She shook her finger at him.

Later they laughed about it, saying she must have forgotten she wasn't in the classroom. But even though he'd boasted of it to Jerry, it worried him; her bravery had been so reckless, and strange as well, because he was certain she'd been more scared at the time than he was. Her fear had exploded, metamorphosed or mutated—a science fiction mouse, fearsomely toothed and vicious. He feels that determination turned now toward him and his illness. He would drop the pillowcase if he had one.

Suddenly he's struck with the odd conviction that it would have been better for their relationship if he'd had one of the deadly cancers. He gets off his hospital bed, picks up the flowers, magazines, and Jerry's get-well card, which is actually a list of porno movies beginning with *Adam and Yves* and ending with *Wicked Waxxx Worxxx*. He stands with his toes on the tape. He flips on the intercom for the nurse.

"Hello? Can you bring me something to put my flowers in?" he says. "How's the weather out there, anyway? Anybody for a game of gin rummy? You could hold all the cards."

/ / /

He comes home from the hospital to an impatient Janice. He thinks this is probably how wives treat husbands who are chronically out of work. She vacuums around him, keeps her own schedule. After he's home for a week, he's sitting at the kitchen table working on a landscaping bid. A woman in Star Valley wants a whole hedge of manzanita. He has offered her sycamore, understanding it is personality she desires, not just ornamentation. Across the table, Janice corrects math papers, circling the wrong answers with an unfriendly black marker.

Wilson says, "Dr. Rodgers's office called to tell me my TSH level is OK. I can stay on the 175 milligrams of Levothyroid."

Janice doesn't look up, just nods. Since he got home, she has quit talking about his cancer, changes the subject when he does. But in her avoidance of it, it is more there than ever, sleeping between them like an untrained dog.

A woodpecker is working on the oak tree outside the window. Native American women harvest the acorns in the fall, make some kind of meal. Wilson turns to glimpse the bird's tweedy back. "How was school?" he says.

This time Janice looks up. "Niki's pregnant," she says.

Wilson says, "Niki? No. How? I mean, oh, I'm sorry."

"Niki said it would be OK, that she loves Joe." Janice pushes the pile of homework papers to one side. "She came up to me in the lunchroom. She was eating a soda cracker, and the only color in her face was the purple under her eyes. She said since she got pregnant she can smell the whole world and the lunchroom odors come to her at different levels, like layered Jell-O: green beans and dirty mop water, with bad teenage hygiene on the bottom. She said, 'Anyway, college can wait.'"

"I'm sorry," Wilson repeats.

Janice picks up her pen and scribbles across the page in front of her, "Label your amplitudes. See me!"

"How will they make it?" Wilson says. "Her father doesn't make anything, does he?" He can see their miserable lives, tarnished promise, shriveled dreams. Suffering is so sneaking, he thinks, and common.

"They can get jobs. They can take turns finishing high school. I don't know. They can write Dear Abby." Her look is level, disappointed, and angry. It includes him, he fears, as well as Abigail Van Buren and thyroid cancer.

"The javelina ate the oak sapling," he says, looking away, "even the pole I used to support it with. A bunch of prints, a whole herd maybe." It distresses him more than he'd realized, the defenseless red oak, the relentlessly destructive javelina.

"It figures" is all Janice says.

"Some people think petunias are the thing to plant," he says uncertainly. "I'm always surprised by that stubborn yucca by the mailbox. It seems so, I don't know, spunky to be surviving under the pines." Next he'll be talking about ants and rubber tree plants. High hopes, he's begging for, or the possibility of them. He's on stage, a comic with bad material, going down, praying for—what else?—Janice's surprised laughter.

"Javelina," he says, "a pig with an attitude."

/ / /

Coming home late from work the next day, Wilson sees Theodora atop the three stacked boulders. He thinks the bizarre-looking cat and the boulders don't in any way belong in the same world. Yet in her grudge-holding, he sees she is as impassive as the rocks she stands on. She is Janice's cat, he thinks with a shudder that feels like a premonition.

He looks at the huge rocks. Sometimes at work they get a call from someone wanting boulders to bunch around the pool or to embed by the driveway. Jerry will yell, "Call Pioneer Gravel! We can't be hauling those monsters around!"

The boulders glow reddish gold where they catch the setting sun. In their shadowed surfaces the color is cool and somber. Despite their mass, they are unformed, remote as the age they came from.

Pulling up to the cabin he finds Janice packed to leave him. He's not surprised, though sorrow deadens and weights his legs and fear enters with each breath.

"Sue says I can stay in their travel trailer until I find a place of my own," she says, carrying her old sewing machine onto the redwood deck, the screen door slamming in exclamation behind her.

Her possessions are a pile of liquor boxes filled with books and clothes, the bamboo lamp she brought into the marriage, her Sea Mist shampoo. He thinks he's never seen a more heartbreaking sight than the *Teachers Add Up* mug balancing on top of her green hot rollers.

"Why?" he says, looking down at his cowboy boots, the stupid happy loops on the toes.

"I can't take it anymore," she says.

"Take what, Janice?"

"You don't get it, do you?" she says.

It's about his illness, maybe Niki, too. Maybe it's about the porno movie titles, which don't seem so funny now, but mean and sad. He knows that mostly it's the cancer that's gotten to her. Gets that much, but he can't stand here and say, "You're leaving me because I have cancer." He can't even think it, really, what it would mean about her or him, them together, and even what it would mean about his cancer.

"Janice, I can try harder." But what would he do? Quit kidding around with Jerry? Paint the garage? Try to be healthy?

"Try harder? It's all your trying that's getting to me. You can't ever admit things are bad. You and your love for nature!" She flings her arms open so wildly, he thinks maybe her anger is at God or Nature. She's backing away from him, then running down the steps into the road that leads toward the cream and red cliffs of the Mogollon Rim. She kicks at the dirt, setting off a small plume of pink.

"Janice," he calls, following her. He remembers now how she wanted to knock over the boulders, how she can't stand not knowing if they will fall or waiting for it to happen.

She stops by the yucca that bends in a spiky bow toward the

mailbox. "I can't take this," she says. She tilts her head back as if she were looking for rain, but she isn't seeing the generous white clouds or the yellow of the hooded oriole. "This will go on and on," she says, "until—"

"I have cancer," he says suddenly. He touches his scar, the smooth ridge blending into the other skin. "I may die." He says it to make her stay, but when he says it again, it is because it is so. "I may die," he says, feeling a cold chill. He looks around, startled. A crow perches in a Douglas fir, ducks its head, lifts its wing. A chipmunk sitting on its haunches fretfully gnaws an acorn.

When he looks back at Janice, he sees a strange peace has transformed her face. He's a student who's finally discovered the solution to the equation.

"That's right," she says solemnly. "You might die."

He thinks she may stay, now that he has admitted defeat. But his loss is so absolute he blinks repeatedly, sensing he has given away something bigger than anything he knew he owned.

"Will you come home?" he says.

Her answer is to take his hand. There is tenderness there, and, yes, warmth.

Farming Butterflies

As Todd hangs car keys on his mother's PROUD PARENT OF CAMELBACK HONOR STUDENT key holder, this is what he suddenly knows about his Aunt Deirdre: she can unflinchingly say the name of the most private body part or reveal anything—that her father wore Youth Dew perfume or that she once lost eleven pounds on a grapefruit and horseradish diet—that she can announce her most raw secrets with abandon, according to mysteries of mood or logic or whim. Lately Todd has begun to suspect women of having frequent bouts of whim. His mother's emphatic fancies, Alisha's rehearsed impulsiveness.

Aunt Deirdre is also not really his aunt, but his mother's closest friend, just arrived for a visit with the family. Right now she's telling him she's famished. She'd like something colorful to eat. Orange circus peanuts or rainbow sherbet. "Joyful food," she calls it. Her nose wrinkles in anticipation, a not unpleasant nose, but the kind where you notice the nostrils first—a little rounder than most people's. Her eye makeup is complicated. Todd has counted three colors—easily—in shades of a healing bruise.

"I think we have some Creamsicles," he says. Then, "Help

yourself," which is a formality, because she's already doing just that: unloading hot peppers, mashed potatoes, and deviled eggs from the refrigerator. She kicks the door shut, and Todd watches the Pizza Barn magnet slide toward the floor. Next to it the library overdue notice and the dry-cleaning receipt shudder and then flap.

She says, "Imagine how much better spinach would taste if it were hot pink!" Then, pausing in mid-lick of the paprika on a deviled egg, she says worriedly, "Is your mom really skinny?"

One of the few things Todd learned about women in high school is how they can trick you with questions. Todd considers, not what the truth might be, but how he can say what Deirdre wants to hear without being disloyal to his mother—though he has only the vaguest idea of what his mother's relative skinniness might be.

"I don't know," he says. Shrugs. Her look—pleased, he can tell from the way her jaw relaxes, though she's still focused on her egg—tells him it's the right answer. He looks out the sliding glass door. In the backyard, starlings are fighting over wind-fallen figs. The deceptively cool-looking swimming pool water flashes hot glints of desert light. The blue sky is pale, as if exhausted from the heat.

Todd circles each of the brass rivets in his jeans pockets with his thumbs, a weird ritual he's found he does when he's nervous. He pulls the chain for the ceiling fan and hears a slight complaining sound underneath the hum. Deirdre's presence feels large and sticky. Not just because of the food all over the table, but there's something uncontained and risky about her, like sitting behind Lizzy Stocks in American Government and watching the straining outline of her bra hooks. Anxiety, but also shamefaced interest, even hope.

Deirdre spreads mayonnaise on seven-grain bread and then plops on a handful of hot peppers, saws the mess in two, takes a bite. The whole unappetizing sight makes the hair on the back of Todd's neck stand up.

Deirdre kicks off broken-down espadrilles and tosses them into the family's shoe pile by the door to the garage. "I've been on the road forever," she says. "When your mom and I were young we were always looking for a road trip. One day we got Mount Rushmore into our heads from watching Rocky and Bullwinkle. We left that afternoon. Rocky the Flying Squirrel, for crying out loud." She airplanes her arms, soaring like Rocky into some memory Todd hopes desperately not to hear, because his mom's behavior now is so relentlessly spontaneous and frequently inappropriate he can only imagine what it must have been like before she was someone's mom. *Now* his mom will shop for and buy a car in a single afternoon—last time, an extremely used yellow Mustang convertible. *Now* his mom walks half-naked from the bathroom to her bedroom, talks about her breasts, calls them "breasts" to show her "emerging awareness of her dignity as a woman." What happened back then when she was gallivanting around with Deirdre is certainly more than he wants to know. *Gallivanting*. Now he's *thinking* like them.

The ceiling fan is kicking up all the refrigerator's notices: a car wash coupon, the dentist's phone number, the phone bill. They flutter; they taunt.

"Should I call her at the hospital and see what time she'll be home?" he says. His mother works in the billing department at

Good Sam. Her hours are the most regular part of her, but calling her would give him something to do besides standing here waiting for some embarrassing or frightening revelation of Deirdre's.

"The hospital! What drama." Deirdre peels fibers off a stick of celery. The strings curl like green hair. She dangles them in her mouth, wraps her tongue around them.

Deirdre looks like a vocabulary word, *precarious.* And she looks like sex too, not the sleek, sexy kind of Hannah Reed, but something harsh and natural and a bit reckless. Hannah Reed and her long, golden red hair are a closed mystery, while Deirdre is a messy open secret, offering answers to questions Todd would rather not know.

He realizes Deirdre is saying something about cactus. "How can you not love the too-little yellow flower hats on a saguaro or a prickly pear shaped like green, thorny pancakes? Affectation and character—in *plants!* Did your parents tell you why I'm visiting? That I lost my job?"

Todd's parents are diligently, exhaustingly honest with their children. He and Alisha were given sex talks with diagrams. Todd's certain it is part of what's wrong with him, that his parents were too open. He suspects them of being calculating as well. For what better way to frustrate a boy's sexuality than by being explicit about sex? But his parents are also forgetful and spotty in what they remember to tell their children about routine matters such as motivations and schedules. He didn't know about Deirdre's job. Hell, he didn't even know she was coming until this morning when his mother asked him to rearrange his pool cleaning jobs to go pick her up.

"It was my fault they fired me," she says. "Sometimes I forgot to go in. I was helping my boyfriend farm butterflies. Painted Ladies. Orange and black. Pretty, but only in a bridesmaidish way. We had problems: poor quality feed, fluctuations in incubator temperatures. Then the eggs began hatching too soon, in the shipments. We were calling experts from all over. Until finally we found one in Minnesota who agreed to come out." Deirdre pauses and takes a dainty bite of her sandwich, chews it carefully. "What happened was she and Brian went off together. Flew away." She flaps her arms, this time like a butterfly. "Left me with six thousand butterflies in various stages of maturity. Can you imagine?"

Of course, he cannot imagine, not this or several other things, like why she's telling him about her love life or even why someone would farm butterflies. She doesn't make sense. Or the sense she makes is as unhelpful as his mother and father's. His father wants to tell him about condom use. Deirdre wants to tell him about betrayal. And all he really wants to know about any of that stuff is what to say to Hannah Reed on the phone now that school's out.

He looks imploringly at the oven's digital clock, trying to figure out when either of his parents might return. He thinks his unhappiness at being a high school graduate enrolled for the fall at the community college pales in comparison to Deirdre's misery or even the misery of playing her host.

Deirdre licks her finger and presses it down on some sandwich crumbs, then brings it to her mouth. "After Brian left, his absence started to grow like a weed in bad science fiction. Bothersome and indestructible, too. And then having those butterflies. Having to let them go. That didn't help me one bit."

Todd wonders why she doesn't ask him about his job or

school. *Something*. It's as if she doesn't know what adults and teenagers are supposed to talk about. She turns her chair around and straddles it. The fiddle-back his mother refinished with a kitchen sponge and turquoise paint is between her legs. Her gauzy skirt hikes up worrisomely on either side.

"I called your mom right after I was fired. She invited me to come for a visit. I was helpless, just sucked up her sympathy like a hummingbird at a feeder."

This absolutely forces Todd to say, "Did you know I play the trombone? Trombone." He works an imaginary slide, the final phrase from the school fight song, then drops his hands defenselessly in his lap.

Deirdre rests her chin on the chair back. "Ump-pah-pah," she says. "Your mom told me. Were you a band nerd or just a cool guy who appreciated music early and had the maturity not to mind getting stuck with the school band stigma?"

"Actually, a band nerd," he says.

It's a small exchange, not much of a joke, but she gets it. Her smile is happy and wide enough to show a mouthful of teeth—teeth his mother says Deirdre used to open beer bottles with. He feels the surprise of a connection, one of those understanding links he assumed he'd always have with Alisha because they are twins. Momentarily, he feels as if he fits again, all awkward six feet of him. He's unexpectedly grateful.

"Deirdre," his father yells, coming in the door. He drops his beat-up accordion briefcase, and he and Deirdre do a hip-bumping, patty-cake thing that is so embarrassing Todd has to look at his sneakers.

"Hasn't Todd grown?" his father says. His father is, as usual, delighted with the most obvious observations.

/ / /

Since graduation, Todd's been sifting and weighing and probing the experience, trying to make it feel more important than it does. He thinks—hopes—you shouldn't slip through something as big as graduation unchanged and unguided. He's scrutinized the black-haired newscaster's commencement speech, but all he can remember is some story about a guy naked under his graduation gown, and he can't even remember the point of that.

One moment during graduation *has* stayed with him, but it's so weird he's not entirely sure it happened or entirely sure he wants it to have happened. It occurred as he was playing his trombone and marching to his place on the apex of Camelback band's sloppy triangle. There was a slide in the fight song, a slide he'd played—at how many football and basketball games?—but this time it was different. He remembers extending his arm with a smooth, steady grip and feeling his soul somehow go with it—a follow-through beyond the brass reach of trombone, beyond the aluminum bleachers, beyond where he was or where he's been. Reality seemed to slip. He's suddenly on a San Francisco street corner, his trombone case open, a few dollars rustling in the worn gray velveteen, the brim of a gentle fedora shading his concentration-closed eyes. He's playing "Mood Indigo," each phrase ending perfectly, opening to the rich surprise of the next. Freed from all clumsy technique, lifted into expansive expressiveness, he plays as he's only dreamed. His breath becomes music.

It's his imagination, he knows that. But it's clearer and feels more relevant than anything that really happened that evening. Now sometimes, while he's driving from pool to pool, he'll see the layered gray of a San Franciscan sky or a Chinese character in pink neon, flashing in a black reflection of plate glass, like a reminder or a sign. He feels foolish. He'd die if anyone knew, but it's so vivid. It scares and thrills him, a mysterious possible life, so exact in detail it must in some way be prophetic.

/ / /

Alisha, who his mother has never tired of pointing out was his "womb-mate," has taken up with the drama club crowd. For some reason this seems to have cured her childhood stuttering, though now she is prone to repeat whole phrases, trying out different inflections and hand gestures. Todd thinks the stuttering was preferable. As babies, they sucked each other's thumbs and scratched each other's ant bites, but now Alisha has turned inward.

She is sunning by their swimming pool, though the only result Alisha gets from her tanning is an occasional swollen forehead. Todd used to call her Alisha the Beluga Whale when that happened, and she'd just throw her ice pack at him. Now he wouldn't dare say anything. She's unpredictable: hostile one day about the style of sunglasses he's wearing, tearful the next about lard in bean burritos. Todd brushes down the sides of the pool. Alisha sweats dramatically. Music comes from the headset of her Sony Walkman, insect voices whining about last chances of last dances. She takes off the headset, shades her eyes, squints at him. "Todd, you're beige." It's an accusation.

"Well, I find it goes with a lot of things."

"But you're outside all day. Why don't you get a tan? Are my eyes the same color as yours? Yours are blue-green." She says this with distaste, presumably because his eyes are neither one color nor the other. Alisha has begun to notice many dissatisfying things. There's a palm frond shadow across her leg, the silhouette of a giant comb.

"How're you liking Aunt Deirdre?" he says.

"I don't know how many of those dinners I can take."

Dinner *had* been wild. Their dad served his Bianca Florentine Lasagna, a towel over his arm in a corny waiter imitation. Their mom told Deirdre about the patient at the hospital who told a nurse she couldn't breast-feed yet because the doctor hadn't been in to poke the holes in her breasts. Then after mentioning that Todd had graduated in the top 5 percent of his class, their parents asked them to tell Deirdre about their college plans.

Todd had looked to Alisha to go first, but she wouldn't look up from the exclamation point she was making with salad croutons.

"I thought Mom was particularly ridiculous," Alisha says now.

For the first time in a long while, he sees they agree. It comforts him, in an old thumb-sucking way.

The beach towel Alisha lies on covers a multitude of rips in an old lounge chair. Her hair is fanned above her head. She speaks with her eyes shut, looking like a severe fortune-teller. He's tempted to ask her advice about Hannah. To ask if Hannah's lowered blond eyelashes are a good or bad sign. To ask if Hannah's laugh—like a car changing gears—is for him or about him.

Alisha says, "Did you see those pills she took? I think they're illegal."

"I doubt that."

"They're something *very* illegal," she says again, her chin up. Alisha likes to shock. When he doesn't respond, she opens one challenging eye. And he knows with a sad dip of regret that whatever he says will extinguish their fragile camaraderie.

"I think," he says, savoring the impossible simplicity of his hope, "she's just having a rough time right now."

"She's surfing for God on the Internet. She thinks she's descended from Anasazi Indians. 'Something has happened—what is it?' Blanche in *A Streetcar Named Desire.*"

He suspects much of what Alisha says is to enable her to quote someone. He can feel the heat of the cool deck through his sneakers, like a warning. He remembers when they were kids cutting out pictures from *Better Homes and Gardens* of rooms they would build in their house when they grew up: ice cream parlor attics and billiard room basements.

"Anyway, it's too bad she lost her job," he says. He kicks a rotting orange. It is bloated and gray like a dead animal.

"I got my dorm assignment," Alisha says. She's headed north in the fall, into the mountains. She is so feverishly thrilled by it, he knows his unhappiness about the community college is genuine. "I want to get some Broadway posters framed," she says. "And a *real* coat."

On one knee, he scoops some water into the test kit tubes. Alisha's plans exhaust him, or not precisely the plans themselves, but the surety of them. Another mystery: how does anyone know so clearly what to do? He adds solution number four to the testing tube, shakes it to see the red swirl turn the water pink. He could do it without testing. Today the pool needs what it needed Monday and the Friday before, what it always needs: twelve ounces of muriatic acid.

/ / /

It's arranged for Todd to take Deirdre on his swimming pool rounds. "Show her the ropes," his father had said. "Or I guess with swimming pool cleaning, it's show her the brushes." And his mother said, "It'll do you some good, Deirdre, to get out into that hot desert you like."

They were watching television news about a divorce lawyer's trial for beating up his client's ex-wife.

His dad turned his face toward Todd, but kept his eyes on the tearful attorney. "Tomorrow's OK, isn't it, Todd?"

"You deserve everything you're getting, buster," his mother said, hiking her chin to the lawyer, but it might as well have been to Todd.

Only Deirdre, he saw, was looking at him, smiling a shy smile, a blushing bride smile.

He looked desperately to Alisha. She glanced up from her hands, lined up finger to finger in steeples, and grinned with savage innocence.

"Dad," he says later, when he finds his father in the bathroom brushing his teeth, "I don't think it'll work for me to take Aunt Deirdre. You know, it's really hot. She's not used to it." He does not add that she's a time bomb.

His father's stomach hangs over the waistband of his pajamas, sags in a truly disheartening way. He brushes his teeth as if he's filming an instructional tape for the American Dental Association. "Son," he says—and how Todd hates to be called that—"Deirdre needs help getting her life back on course. Can't you just take her around? Stop and buy her a taco." He rinses his mouth. "My treat," he says, because life is so simple for his father, Todd thinks, that he really supposes someone can be bought these days for the price of lunch.

His parents have always treated their children like adults, which his friends have unwittingly called cool, because they had no idea of its obligations. You can't make another kid understand the burden of an unlocked liquor cabinet or the ordeal of twenty-four-hour-a-day access to adult cable channels. "We trust you," his parents said over and over, until Todd wanted to scream, "Please don't. I think I might be a maniac."

But the worst of it was he and Alisha weren't maniacs. They *acted* like adults—parents, in fact—waiting up while their father and mother danced all night at the Rocking Horse Saloon.

His father now forms exaggerated vowel sounds with his mouth. He claims these are toning exercises for his neck. "*A-E-I-O-U*," he says. Lost, Todd walks out.

But later he passes the glassed-in patio and hears the hiccup of a sob. He sees Deirdre in the room, sitting at a small desk. Her back is to him, hunched as if protecting something. "Please," she says into the phone. "Brian, it'll be different." A pause. "I know, but I'll quit that. I promise." She strokes a geranium's jointed stem. Drops it. "But Brian—" Her words are cut off by her weeping. She nods, accepting, admitting whatever she's being accused of.

Todd has never heard such anguish, didn't realize it really existed. He thinks of his mother's grief at his grandmother's death, dignified and contained. And though Alisha evidences misery, it is as posed and vain as a party dress. Deirdre's sorrow is homely and unbounded. It seems to soar, a pain set free by hopelessness.

In his bedroom, he closes the door with both hands on the knob, carefully, tightly.

In the morning, Todd keeps glancing at Deirdre, worrying about how she's holding up, whether breakdowns are like David Andrew's epileptic seizures or like Jason Reily's diabetic lows. Would he even recognize a breakdown?

But Deirdre seems content, pleased with the day. His beat-up

Nissan truck doesn't have much in the way of shocks and has no air-conditioning. She sticks her arm out the window, pats the side. "I wish we had some Jethro Tull on the eight-track and some beer in the back. Then we'd be like a couple of teenagers."

One of them actually *is* a teenager, he thinks, and he has no idea what an eight-track might be. But he's glad—and relieved—she feels better. He considers telling her about Mr. Petersen, his newly divorced biology teacher, maybe even setting her up with him.

When they pull up to a huge Spanish colonial, Deirdre hops out and carries the long-handled brush and net while he totes his bucket of chemicals and test kit.

"Will you look at this?" she says.

The pool, with its tiers of blue and white tile and twisted columns, resembles a Turkish harem. Todd fills containers like miniature buoys with jumbo chlorine tablets while Deirdre flicks away leaves slimy with pool water. She talks about her high school summers working at a hardware store, how she'd loved the names for toggle bolts and wing nuts. "Your mom had a more glamorous job," she says. "She worked at a Dairy Queen in a tight white uniform."

He sees his mother's past hovering over his own. Homecoming Queen Gives Birth to Band Nerd. He wonders what she does with her disappointment in him. He imagines it in the form of the impossible jewelry his father gives her—the brass fertility goddess earrings that she exclaimed over before they disappeared. Todd thinks she did something similar when he failed to even apply to a university. She shoved her discouragement into some drawer and pulled out something else to wear. Her proud mother badge. He wonders if it fools her.

Deirdre says, "Your mom says you have a girlfriend."

His scalp tingles. His wet hands sweat. Could his mom have guessed about Hannah?

"A flutist?" Deirdre says.

"Jenny? No, she's just a friend." In addition to a rather unsuccessful evening at the Sadie Hawkins dance with Jenny Allen, there was only a movie gang date. But besides being a flutist, Jenny is a poet. Though his mother doesn't read poetry, she's confident only worthwhile people write it.

"I'm certain I've got some bad love advice if you need it," Deirdre says.

"No," he says, quickly, stunned and shy at the invitation. "Anyway, I mostly like to figure out my own stupid stuff to do."

They nod together, almost in sync, a relaxed rhythm, as Todd brushes the sides of the pool.

"Probably better that way," Deirdre says. Then, "How come I haven't heard you play the trombone?"

"I don't usually play much in the summer," he says, though it isn't true. He's quit playing altogether—just at the point when he feels he's becoming more accomplished—because he fears the music will give him away. Atonal and unusually metered, it sounds confused and searching.

Deirdre pulls at the elastic of her gray jogging shorts. Todd thinks she will tan today, her skin color deepening with a cheap, alluring glow. He hands her the brush and nods toward the opposite side of the pool.

She says, "Are you going to play in the band when you get to college?"

He taps his jeans rivets. He thinks of sitting in the bleachers at football games, his music clipped to the stand with clothespins. "I don't know if I'm going to college in the fall," he says, for the first time speaking the truth of it and startled by his confession.

"When I graduated from high school I went to wax museums. Ten of them." She holds up all ten fingers. "There was one in Denver for women rodeo riders. Another one in Las Vegas had Marilyn Monroe's mole on the wrong side."

The Polaris vacuum cleaner makes a robotic patrol of the pool bottom. The sweep hose whips.

"I keep thinking about going to live in San Francisco for a while and just messing around with my music, seeing what happens." He's surprised how easy it was to say, how saying it makes it seem actually possible, but most of all he's surprised that Deirdre doesn't look surprised. She nods, or he wouldn't have been certain she'd heard at all. "I know it's a stupid idea. It probably won't work out." He has to say this, someone has to.

Deirdre slaps the back of her neck with pool water. "Well, you can't do something like that and still be a card-carrying band nerd, that's for sure," she says. She smacks her lips, a sound like approval. "But your mom and dad *are* going to kill you."

"Yeah, but first they'll talk me to death. They'll say how they know I'll make the right decision. They know I'll do what's best. They *trust* me."

She smiles. A breeze hot as a blow-dryer makes the palms sway obsequiously.

Todd says, "My parents won't accept failure. What chance do I have for any real success?"

Deirdre clears her throat. "I could go with you," she says. "It's not as if I have anything to go back to."

A construction wrecking ball, Todd sees in this, aimed at his parents' hearts. The only thing, he supposes, more worrisome to them than his going off to San Francisco alone would be his going off to San Francisco with Deirdre. It delights him.

"I'd get a job working for Ghirardelli chocolates," Deirdre says. "Don't you love those chocolate molds? Seashells, golfers, Scottie dogs. They have a trombone one too, don't they?"

"A road trip," Todd says.

"I know about road trips." Deirdre sits and puts her feet into the pool. Her sneakers must slurp up the water. "I've always done whatever came into my head and sometimes—often—it doesn't work out. But you can't be Alisha's womb-mate forever. Right?"

He sees himself stepping off a curb onto a gray wobble of cobblestone. He steadies a soft package of white butcher paper, smelling the sweet stink of fish. Deirdre walks along the curb, dipping a foot like a kid on a wall, balancing a basket on her head. Then she stops, turns to him, and laughs Hannah's laugh, the sounds of shifting from first all the way through fourth gears. It welcomes him; it embraces him; it convinces him: this bright laugh of adventure.

/ / /

After cleaning eight pools, after watching his mother nearly swoon with horror and Alisha nearly swoon with jealousy at the sight of Deirdre's fierce sunburn, Todd is trying to sleep when he hears his mother and Deirdre talking. He looks through the tangerine tree outside his window and sees their legs, ghostly in the underwater pool light, weaving like bleached seaweed.

"I guess I thought butterflies were romantic, Debbie," Deirdre says, leaning into the water and fluttering her hands like a shadow-puppet butterfly. "I thought they were some kind of sign, an ancient Asian symbol of happiness."

His mother points her toe and brings it up out of the water. Silver droplets splash back into the lit pool. "Deirdre, you make too much of signs. Butterflies are, after all, insects." In her swimming suit, he sees his mother *is* skinnier than Deirdre. Fleetingly, Todd wishes he'd told Deirdre his mother wasn't skinny.

His mom says, "Deirdre, farming butterflies was the least of Brian's gambling. He drank too much. He was not a nice man."

"He was pigeon-toed," Deirdre says, helplessly. "How can a pigeon-toed man really be bad?"

Todd knows Deirdre won't mention San Francisco, though he finds he wishes she would. He can feel the tight tugging heat of her sunburn. She and his mother face each other in the water. He sees they are their own kind of womb-mates; a complex affinity balanced on something as opposite as a magnet's polarity. What are the allowances his mother makes for her friend? With him she's always looking for something to be proud of.

"Deirdre," his mother says. She pushes Deirdre's hair off her forehead. It is a mother gesture, but not a gesture of his mother's. "You're going to be OK, Deirdre." Then she swims toward the deep end.

"I don't want to go to college," Todd whispers to her swimming form. She floats on her back, brings her arms out of the water with surprising gracefulness, and he imagines her saying to him, "You're going to be OK, Todd."

/ / /

In a room without shadows, black dark, or brilliant light, Todd plays with Duke Ellington's band. In the dream, Johnny Hodges is on alto saxophone, Jimmy Hamilton on clarinet. Weaving cigarette smoke filters the stage lights uncertainly, as Todd plays the blue note, filling his lungs until they ache. Sweat trickles down the small of his back.

Todd is unfamiliar with the score. It has a pleading quality, a question that makes his perspiration chill. Then suddenly he's playing solo for Hannah Reed, a bright phrase now, clear, but melting. He's amazed by his technique, effortless and magical, a glorious flight of sound. But imploring tones continue from somewhere else, with a human voice that must be the sax. Then the music becomes language, his mother's voice. "Todd, please wake up. There's an emergency. I have to go with Dad and Deirdre. The hospital. Do you understand?" He opens his eyes to his mother, confused by the hall light that silhouettes her.

"Yeah," he says, not sure what he's agreed to.

/ / /

He's surprised to find his mother in the kitchen in the morning. She's in a tattered white robe he hasn't seen for a while, holding a mug of coffee in both hands. Her smile is overbright. "Deirdre's going to be all right. An overdose. She didn't mean to, an accident really." Her nodding is to make it true. "They have to keep her. You know?"

She picks up a spoon, stirs her coffee with a brisk clatter. "I've been thinking of the time Deirdre and I went to Mount Rushmore." She looks into the backyard, studying it as if it's the Great Plains of South Dakota. "We panned for Black Hills gold and ate buffalo jerky. I have a picture where I'm scalping her with a rubber tomahawk. We're a couple of skinny girls. But Mount Rushmore—" She taps the spoon on her palm, then holds it tightly still. "We got there after dark, sneaked in after the park was closed. And on top of the monument, by the presidents' foreheads, Deirdre walks over and looks down. Her sandal toes hang over and she says, 'Whew, this would be just too easy.' She leans over, and I see how dangerous it is—she is. I tell her to stop it right now. 'Come away from there, Deirdre!'" His mother's plea is sad, frightened, and filled with the anger only found in profound love. "Please," she says, quietly now to Todd. Her hair falls into her face. It's *his* hair, Alisha's and his, beige and bent in waves that don't curve regularly. The loose strand of hair scares him.

She puts the spoon down. "Deirdre's going to be fine."

But Todd knows she isn't. He feels a witness to her death, just as his mother has witnessed her past. Whether it's from pills or heights or cars or guns, it will come down to the same lost gamble: venturing too near to an edge. Some too-close attention to cactus or brightly colored food or butterflies.

His mother says, "If Deirdre would just—" But she doesn't continue. She reties the belt on the ratty robe and looks away.

Todd says, "I'm going to the hospital."

"No, not now." She says his name. Just his name. He hears the sharp *t,* the stop of the *d,* nothing more.

He drives to the hospital with an odd precision, carefully signaling lane changes, braking to gentle stops.

Heartbreak House

"Welcome to heartbreak house," I say to my husband Jack.

He looks over the magic wand he's holding above some sailboats-in-the-Bahamas playing cards and says, "It's *hotel.*"

Whatever. We're talking about our teenager, Claire.

I say, "She's talking about jumping, slashing, *and* swallowing."

The eight of diamonds rises from the coffee table, responding, presumably, to Jack's magic wand. I hate card tricks; I never understand how I'm supposed to have been tricked.

"She's morose, distraught, despairing," I say.

Jack says, "Does she know how to be all those things?" His hairline begins low on his forehead. It makes him look capable but simple; as if he can lift heavy things but not necessarily know when to put them down.

"All Claire knows is Ben had a date," I say.

Jack says—and I can't blame him—"Oh, not again."

"Will you talk to her? Tell her boys are beasts."

"Boys are beasts," he says, considering. Then he curls his lip, an Elvis Presley snarl, and shuffles the cards.

I find Claire slouched in front of the TV, melted into the sofa.

She's wearing a baggy gray sweatsuit—being ugly is important at a time like this. A few brown curls have worked themselves free from her ponytail. They tell the truth, she's a pretty girl, even if her looks—wide almond-shaped eyes and bowed lips—veer toward something more interesting than Pleasant Hills High School. Now she is eating M&M's with chopsticks. On the TV, a fresh-faced Audrey Hepburn is singing "Moon River" despite a slight VCR tracking problem.

"How's it going?" I say.

The last time Ben went out with another girl, the two of them rode a block of ice down Grandview Hill and drank hot chocolate with sprinkles at her house. These and several other sordid details were provided to Claire by the other girl's friend, proving her greater loyalty to Claire. That's when Claire started watching *Breakfast at Tiffany's*. Now when we hear Audrey stumbling up her apartment stairs we know—like when Claire was younger and there was a croupy cough in the night: trouble.

"How about going to get something to eat?" I say.

Claire's parrot, Mrs. Paul, screams from Claire's room, "Barney, you've lost your gun? Again?"

"I hate him," Claire says.

"What's not to hate?"

"Oh, you don't really hate him," she says.

I forget, whatever my reservations are about Ben—that he nudges his food onto his fork with his thumb, that he rides his motorcycle onto my lawn—whenever they have problems, in her mind I'm on his side.

I say, "You could ask someone else out yourself."

"Mom, there's no one else to ask out." She throws down her chopsticks, scoops up a handful of M&M's, turns resolutely to watch Audrey Hepburn—now talking to Peppard on the fire escape. Her winsome friendliness will inspire him to start writing again.

"Honey," I say, "there's a boy on every corner, like a bus stop. God made lots of them. Tons."

"I don't *want* a boy," she says. "I hate them." She's off to her room, stopping for what sounds like corn chips and salsa. Doors and cupboards slam.

Outside Jack is pruning the blossoming thundercloud tree. Over the years, he's planted our yard with the weekend specials from Tip Top Nursery: the box elder, the red maple, the Russian olive.

"I've tried," I tell him.

"Tried?"

"Claire. I've talked to her."

Jack says, "Claire *wants* to be miserable. She wants us all to be miserable. If we aren't miserable, Claire can't be sure she's miserable." With a flourish, he presents me with a twig of thundercloud. Pink blossoms leapfrog up the stem. "Misery is the truest part of love. It lets you know that you are."

"In love or miserable?"

"Both."

Jack talks like this, in rambling, blurry truths. Wait a minute, I'm always thinking. But he doesn't wait—hasn't, won't.

He'll say: "Love is like driving a car blindfolded."

I'll say: "Hit and run?"

He'll say: "Hit *or* run."

"An apricot tree," he says now. "Wouldn't it be nice to plant an apricot tree over there by the apple tree? Then we could have some of that apricot jam with pecans my mom makes." He smiles, takes off his Caterpillar cap, and wipes his forehead on the shoulder of his ragged plaid shirt. He does this thing with his eyebrows: makes them go up with pretend surprise, but underneath is childlike delight, as if I've brought home a treat from the grocery store. It gets me when he does that, always has. Something about it, maybe the innocence that isn't so innocent; or the pleasure that is.

He looks up into the coloring-book blue sky—a wide sky capping the mountains of the Wasatch Range. Over his shoulder I see our neighbor, Terry, barefooted, walking gingerly toward us. She's always reminded me of the prettier one of some twins I went to high school with, girls who parlayed a one-handed walkover into a way of life. Terry has long, bouncy curls, like a bunch of yo-yos. She's a little younger than I am so her bottom hasn't begun to slide down the back of her legs. It's kind of bouncy, too, come to think of it, which is probably good since her husband left several months ago to work some shady deal in Kuwait where he only calls on the first Sunday of the month and whispers, "I haven't a clue where this will all end."

Terry says, "You guys seen Miles?" That's her cat.

"Un-uh," we say, careful not to look at each other, because while we *haven't* seen Miles, yesterday we saw a ball of black fluff. Just the sort of stuff a coyote will leave behind.

"Damn," she says. She sits down by a row of red tulips and pulls a thorn out of her foot, the kind like a miniaturized death star. She pushes her peppy hair out of her eyes, but it's back in her face immediately. There's a bruise on her leg at the height of a lowered dishwasher door. She's always banging her head on cupboards; somehow I know it.

Jack says, "I could help you look for him."

"What?" I say.

He shrugs. "Her cat?"

"Would you?" Terry says. "He hasn't been home since yesterday. I'm so worried."

Jack nods sympathetically. His cap has left a red band across his forehead. There are a few pink blossom petals on his shoulder.

"Let me just get the garbage can out to the street," he says.

Terry hobbles along beside him. "Maybe I'd better get some shoes," I hear her say.

In her room Claire is feeding Mrs. Paul. The bird is a red-sided parrot, colored like a Superman costume. Claire inherited it from my brother Patrick, who had come to resent the mocking cheerfulness in its whistling "The Andy Griffith Show" after his boyfriend moved out. The birdseed smells like musty fruit.

Last year when Claire felt she'd outgrown it, she stripped off her bed's white eyelet canopy. Now the wire form arches in raw nakedness above an olive drab army blanket. A poster of Smokey Bear looks down imploringly on a huge pile of wadded clothes, both clean and dirty. The room looks like violence.

"How can you tell which clothes are dirty and which are clean?" I say.

"Mom, the ones I've worn are the dirty ones." Then, "Did I tell you who it was?" She has Jack's habit of beginning in mid-thought. "Mindy Stone." She stutters slightly on the *s*, and I remember how she said, "Dale Steadman," when he tore the Ms. Fix-It badge off her Girl Scout uniform. There's a salsa stain like a splattered raindrop on the front of her sweatshirt.

"Mindy Stone," I repeat—whoever she is—knowing I've been ordered to hate her.

Mrs. Paul says, "Gol-lee, Aunt Bea." The bird moves in a two-step on its bar. "I sure do love apple pie."

"Can you believe it?" Claire says.

What is hard to believe is her disbelief, especially because Jack believes everyone is capable of everything. "Nixon knew," he said. "So what?" But Claire is one of those people who believe so fervently in justice and fairness she'll always have trouble getting them.

"Can you believe it?" she asks once more and shuffles out of the room to pose the same question to a girlfriend on the phone. I hear her voice, muffled outrage. Apparently the girlfriend knows other outrages that fuel Claire's.

"In the *refrigerator?*" She chokes with indignation.

I pick up some of the clothes she's already worn and start some laundry. The washing machine has a baffling occasional leak that reappears like a family ghost. Today, I mop up the puddle with a dirty towel left over from Jack's earlier car washing.

I remember when Claire was born, how we brought her home from the hospital, amazed they were letting us. Then when she was five days old I got mastitis, a hundred and five fever, and breasts so sore and swollen they felt like a separate life. I realized now I couldn't die, and I saw how before I'd become a mother death had always loomed as a simple, last-ditch option.

I nursed Claire and cried. I feared the red and yellow capsules the doctor had given me were no match for the fierce illness. Helplessly, I entertained thoughts of how sad my funeral would be and how Claire would cry every time Jack's new wife tried to give her a bottle. Then I fell asleep.

I woke to the smell of mother's milk, brown sugary and thin cream with the stinging antiseptic and petroleum jelly odor of Bag Balm. Light filtered through the miniblind's slats, across Jack, who stood over me with an armful of assorted socks.

"Sweetheart," he said, "I want to help. What temperature do you wash socks on?"

"It's the color of the clothes, Jack, not the style." I realized I was looking at the only person more frightened than I was. He nodded quickly because he had no idea at all what I'd meant.

Now I empty the water from the washing machine leak next to the dwarf peach tree by the carport. I hear "Mii-les."

Then Terry's feminine echo, "Mii-les."

The split-level house kitty-corner from us has a sheet of plastic over the higher of the roofs, like a shower cap. A goat-sized dog is chained in the front to a lilac bush I expect to see him pulling along behind him any day. In the summer the young son of the family comes over to sell me sweaty pebbles named *Gary* and *Frankie*. Terry walks up the crack in their driveway, carefully, as if she's on a tightrope. She's empty-handed, of course.

Claire comes out. "Can I make this?" She holds up a boxed dessert mix.

"Sure," I say.

But she doesn't go right in. She stays and watches Terry standing on tiptoes in cheat grass, looking over the prickly hedge of the neighboring ranch house.

Claire says, "What's she doing?"

"Looking for her cat."

"The one you said a coyote got?"

"Yep."

Jack is waiting for a beat-up Toyota truck to pass before he crosses the street. He's picked up a couple of littered beer bottles, crosses the street juggling them. When he sees us, he catches them and bows.

"What a dork," Claire says.

Terry joins him on the curb. He points in the direction of Mount Timpanogos. Terry shakes her head. Boing, boing, boing. Then she nods, sits down, takes off her sneakers, and shakes something out.

"What's Dad doing?" Claire says.

"Helping her look for the cat."

"Mom?" Claire says.

"Hm?"

"Want to know what I think?"

"Nope." I don't even want to know what I think. I'm hoping it'll go away.

She says, "Want some chocolate French silk dessert?"

In the kitchen Claire sings, "Bake in center of the preheated oven," to the tune of "Moon River."

I say, "Don't you ever wish Audrey Hepburn had just stayed with Buddy Epstein?"

"The 'Beverly Hillbillies' guy?" Appalled, she puts down the package.

"Pa, let's go fishing," Mrs. Paul screams.

Claire says, "What do they mean by a mixing bowl?"

I hand her one.

"Can we leave one of the eggs out?" she says. "Mom, Susie says it was Mindy Stone who did the asking when Ben and her went out."

"He's still scum to have gone."

"Scum," she says. She sticks the beaters in the mixer. They fall out. I push them back in until they click, turn on the oven, and get out a Pyrex measuring cup.

"What should I do?" she says.

"Put it in the bowl."

"About Ben."

"Miles!" I hear through the open window.

"Miiiiiles!"

"Mom?" Claire says.

I stick my head out the window. "Jaaa-k!"

The mixer hums with self-satisfaction.

Outside, standing on the curb, I can't see either Jack or Terry. The neighbor with roofing troubles picks up three days of yellowed newspaper. I wave and nod encouragingly. A motorcycle whizzes by. Too late, I remember to check to see if it's Ben. Lower on the street, it does some gear changing; something that sounds treacherous. But I hear no calls for Miles.

Jack doesn't know how to keep himself out of trouble. He's like my dog when I was a kid. He slept every night for five years on a blue plaid pillow. Then one day he got up and tore it completely apart. My dad and I stood there looking at wads of stuffing and shreds of fabric. "Why did he do that?" I asked.

My dad said, "Most of the time, it's just easier to be stupid."

I go back in the house and hand Claire a spatula, keeping a spoon for myself. I turn off the oven.

"Your father *is* a dork," I say.

We start to eat the chocolate French silk batter, dipping it thoughtfully from the mixing bowl. I stare at the empty box. Claire taps the picture of a maraschino cherry perched seductively atop an avalanche of whipped cream. "Ben says maraschino cherries are indigestible. Every one you've ever eaten stays in your stomach until you die."

She licks the back of her spatula, points it at me. I put down my spoon. She puts down the spatula. We go at the batter with just our fingers.

Claire says, "Why do they go to the trouble to bake things when the batter is always so good?"

The phone rings.

"Hello," Claire says. "I wish," she says. "I guess." She hangs up, smooths the front of her sweatshirt. "The other day, Ben and I, we're going downtown. I'm PMS. Real grouchy. Looking at all the litter: hamburger wrappers, a couple of Styrofoam cups, everything just rolling back and forth in the wind. And it bugs me, so I say to Ben, 'Why do people have to litter when there are garbage cans everywhere? Look,' I say, and I point to this whole row of them against the supports for an overpass, 'six over there.' Then Ben says, 'Are you serious? They fill those with sand. They're crash barriers.' I feel, like, *so* stupid. Know what I say next? 'So? People could *still* use them for trash.'"

She opens a cupboard by the stove, picks up a bag of marshmallows, squeezes it. She says, "That's when I knew I didn't love him."

I say, "Love isn't necessarily based on love."

She nods slowly, licks batter off her knuckle. It takes determination to continue eating. Sweetness oozes out of our pores, slows us down some. I think of how cheesecake makes Jack sweat under his eyes. I push up my sleeves. The front of Claire's sweatshirt looks like a smudge of children's artwork—batter on top of salsa and Coke and other stuff.

"Uncle Patrick," I say, referring to the original parrot owner, "says love isn't flowers and candy. It's quirky little things." Patrick has for years had a crush on Luciano Pavorotti. "It's incredible," he's said, "what that man can convey with a big handkerchief."

"Uncle Patrick is a romantic," my *Breakfast at Tiffany's* addict says with disapproval.

The phone rings.

"Don't answer it," Claire says. She's serious even with chocolate smeared on her chin.

A breeze blows through the open window, a small puff bringing in the popcorn smell of apricot blossoms and the lulling intoxication of early-season lawnmower exhaust.

Claire says, "Susie wants me to go shopping with her for a new bikini. She says her bikini top shrank."

I say, "Just the top?"

"Only the top."

"She wishes."

Claire smiles. "Good one, Mom."

We see Jack and Terry cross back to our side of the street, walking from behind a passing van. They stop by our ginkgo tree. Terry's shoeless again. She's carrying a switch of forsythia, the blossoms fluorescent yellow. Burdock rises like a plume from Jack's cap. He folds up his pocketknife. I hear him say, "Rolled it twice." Terry's response is lost in the roar of a motorcycle Claire jumps up to see.

"Was it him?" I say.

She says, "I don't care if it was." She sits back down. "Ben is scared of snakes." Revealing this makes her feel better. "His brother had his pickup repossessed while he was at Taco Bell." This proves Ben is just human, *and* he has cared for her enough to share his secrets. But then she says, "He's never eaten a green vegetable in his whole life," and a wistfulness sets in that silences her.

I say, "Have you given any more thought about a major next year?"

"I've been thinking of environmental psychology."

"Oh," I say, helplessly.

On the front lawn Jack and Terry begin a tango. Terry clamps the forsythia between her teeth. A tango. Fast steps, slow glides. Jack knows more than just card tricks.

"Miles!" Jack shouts when they change direction.

"Jack!" I yell. He pauses, looks around, finally focusing on the window I'm leaning from. He waves—as grandly as a sports hero—blows me a kiss, then tips Terry backward.

Claire says, "What about Dad, Mom?"

I sigh. "Dad majored in engineering. Have I ever told you how we met in a college geology lab? He had this whitened circle outline of Skoal in the back pocket of his jeans. I was so innocent I thought it might be a condom. He walked gracefully, kind of like a big cat. Dad never brought a pencil to class, sometimes forgot paper, too. Careless. Your father was always a gamble. Then one day he looked at me with—you can't imagine such smoldering eyes. He said, 'You know, it's *igneous* as in *ignite*.' I could just feel the bristle of his short, tough hair. I had to swallow hard. But the only thing I could think to say was '*Sedimentary* as in *sedan*.'"

Claire rolls her beautiful eyes. Dad isn't the only parental dork. But I remember now when I said it, how Jack had arched his eyebrows for the first time. Something in me was plucked or melted or, yes, ignited.

"Mom, Dad's fox-trotting on the front lawn, and he's looking for a woman's dead cat. Doesn't that kind of bother you?"

I say, "All love is some part confidence, some part despair. Anyway, how do you know what to make of what? Uncle Patrick told me about a man he hit it off with in Denver. He told Patrick about his dream house, but when they got there, the carpet was green shag. There were strings of plastic beads over some of the windows. Orange beanbag chairs. Patrick thought, OK, he's bought a fixer-upper. But the guy started explaining how he'd *fixed it up*. He's duplicating the house he grew up in. Room for room, fixture by fixture."

Claire says, "Oh, sick!"

"Patrick said he ran out of there thinking what a nut the guy was. But after he'd been home for a while, he decided maybe it was actually good. So his friend had a happy childhood. What was so bad about that?"

"Uncle Patrick," Claire says, "is a little nuts himself."

Jack and Terry are sitting on the front lawn watching the neighbor boy cross the street toward them. Claire and I quit licking our fingers for a minute to watch.

The neighbor says something to Jack and Terry in a shrill voice about "a tan dog" and "long teeth."

The telephone rings. This time Claire leaps to answer it, runs to take it in the other room.

The little boy points to a spot across the street, then pantomimes a death, killing and being killed both. He wilts to the ground, his eyes tightly shut, his tongue hanging out. Terry looks toward Jack, her hair in her eyes. When she pushes it back, there's the dismay of loss. Jack shakes his head, says something ending in ". . . even for a parrot."

Claire returns to the kitchen. She puts the spoon and spatula slowly into the empty bowl. She grips the bowl's sides, leaving blurred fingerprints on the stainless steel when she lets go. "Mom, it's over with Ben."

I've heard this so many times, my reassuring response is almost automatic, but I'm stopped by something in her face; a grief has hardened the Sophia Loren lips. An ancient sorrow is now fresh. She hasn't said this so I'll dispute it.

She moves carefully, taking the mixing bowl to the sink, watches as tap water fills it. She centers the faucet lever and then the spigot, stops—bewildered at the completion of that small task. Then she nods as if acknowledging her misery.

"I've got to try to get over him," she says. Her sentiment is as huge and necessary as it is hackneyed and difficult—more difficult than she knows, but she is curiously calm. This pain is too serious for dramatics.

"I'm sorry, Claire."

She nods in gracious acceptance.

I can tell her she will get over this. I can tell her there will be others. I can tell her the hurt will end, and someday Benjamin Jeremiah Lewis, with his hopeful brown eyes and fast red motorcycle, won't even enter her mind.

But I don't.

"Uncle Patrick," I say, "has signed up at the Fred Astaire School of Dance. He did it, he says, because he learned to appreciate Fred Astaire's genius one evening watching *Flying Down to Rio* on the late show. He said it just gives him chills what that man can suggest with a top hat."

Claire traces the patterns of the counter tile, easing her finger along the grout. She tries to smile. "I think I'll go change. I'm going to call Susie. See if she'd like to go get something to eat."

"Why not?" I say. *Eat?* I think. Then: Oh, Claire. I would like to tell you about the mastitis, how its penetrating ache filled my body, but also how it expanded my soul. How you slept on my stomach and our breathing mingled and sometimes matched. How I didn't die.

I say, "Honey?"

"I know, Mom," she says, and walks to her room.

Terry and Jack are standing up. Terry is brushing off her butt, which is not as bouncy as I remember. An old station wagon passes with a ladder sticking out of its back window, a red rag tied on the end. A Montgomery Ward delivery van comes from the other direction. The vehicles pass each other like stage curtains parting. In the opening, Miles appears on the opposite curb.

"Mii-les," Terry screams.

"Miles?" Jack says.

Entwined, the cat and his mistress head for home. Miles rests on Terry's neck like a black fur wrap or a lover's arm.

"Jack," I yell out the window, "come in here!"

The eyebrows. Oh, hell. He does the *eyebrows*. "Did you see the *cat?*" he says, as if it's a joke we've been having.

Claire comes out in cutoffs as small as postage stamps. Her hair is brushed, her face is clean. She has the natural heart-stopping grace of girls her age, the grace that accompanies the lack of understanding about its duration.

"I saw David Searing bagging groceries at Albertson's. He's a nice boy," I say.

"Oh, you don't really like him," Claire says.

I think this might be a good sign.

Jumping

This is what never happened.

Kelly and Veronica and I are standing in front of the church waiting for rides home. The boys are chasing each other with their jackets open, even though their faces are red and roughened by the cold. Then childhood's most exuberant exclamation: "You're going to die!" One boy to another, completely true and completely not.

"Yeah, yeah," Kelly says, with a mittened shooing motion, feigning magnificent indifference to hide the awful excitement of girls turning thirteen.

"I think he likes you," I say to Veronica. (Notice, please, my generous compliment. What is more kind than a recognition of someone else's love?)

"Who? Brent?" she says, acting surprised, but I see she's already thought it.

The mothers' car tires slurp through wet snow.

Kelly says, "You'll make a cute couple." Coming from Kelly, this means something. Coming from Kelly, it means you're in.

Veronica's smile always made her look stupid, so when I invent this scene, I can't let her mess it up by smiling. I allow her a contented nod. I want everything to be perfect. When Veronica climbs in her mother's car, cold but happy, I know that it is.

/ / /

It would have happened thirty-three years ago. It would have helped if it—or something like it—had. *If only.* I see it all the time in my work, how small events can change history. I study names, nomenclature: place names, given names, family names, ethnic names, nicknames. A time or two I've been an expert witness. Once I was interviewed on network news. I turn up forgotten information about why baby girls were named Artemisia; why some place was called Maybe. I know the name Wendy first appeared in *Peter Pan,* and the most common name in the world is Mohammed. I've learned the flukiness of names and name-giving. I've seen how a name's viability can be lost because of a bad-apple Judas or Benedict.

I think of Veronica, the ski lift accident, and the time that came after as I've thought of names and naming—a freakish thing that has made all the difference, though I'm still trying to identify what that difference is.

Recently the accident's details started coming back to me—a return like comets or geese. A reentry, an insistent one, like a birth. Parts of what happened then interrupt my day now, insisting I think about it, somehow respect it, understand it matters—I don't know all what. I find myself explaining to my husband Dave a particularity of the ambulance ride—that the sirens were off—or recalling the sky, how the air was truly clear.

"Joan?" he says, curious but patient. "Joan, why are you talking about it now?"

/ / /

They fell from ski lift chairs, and we thought it was just someone throwing garbage.

"What the heck?" Kelly said. We had been taught littering was a crime.

But then we saw: too big, too heavy. They were actually being thrown themselves, launched from their seats, bucked like rodeo riders, tumbled like dice. They fell gracefully downward. Floated on a summer day in tragedy's own slow time.

I said, "Kelly, what should we do?" I rubbed my eyes behind my eyeglasses, a pantomime of disbelief, but how could this be true?

We had been camping with our church group lower on the mountain, and this afternoon we were riding the ski lift to enjoy the view. But now beneath us, ahead and thirty yards farther down the hill, we could see our companions, three girls and our camp leader, lying on the ground. They moved, but it was only a leg or two, lethargic, ineffectual efforts, as if they had all stumbled while drunk.

"Jump," Kelly commanded, "before they start it up again, before it throws us out."

One of the ski lift chairs was wrapped crazily around a huge support beam. The ski lift was disabled. It wouldn't have started, couldn't. I saw that, knew it exactly.

Kelly jumped first, landed in a crouch, steady as a gymnast.

I hung from the footrest twenty-five feet above the ground, looking at aspen trees. Their leaves fluttered encouragingly. The beauty of the day would be remarked on—how it was shattered by tragedy—when our story was reported later on the ten o'clock news. But, of course, nothing was shattered. It was an "America-the-Beautiful" sky: noble and particularly blue.

I later said how I felt it in my stomach, the wind that blew my body slightly just before I let go, but I have no confidence in that now. It may be just part of the story and not part of the truth. I know I counted to five, twice. I remember the hurt and relief of landing.

I called to Kelly. "Wait for me. I'm bleeding." I had fallen forward and scraped my face and bent my glasses. I was desperately afraid of what might happen next—what *did* happen—that she would run down the hill for help. That would leave me to follow, doing . . . but what *would* I do when I got to our companions? I might have counted again before I ran, but I didn't hesitate long. This impresses me, that as a child I faced this, went forward into the mayhem, recognizing there was no way out.

I felt the hot and cold sting of the scrapes on my face. Rocks made the path uneven. I recall stubby milkweed pods and fragile Queen Anne's lace. There was a Utah summer's own dusty, bitter, green smell. But then as I got to where they lay, there was no picture and only one sound. It came when one of them called my name. Linda spoke to me, but I was too frightened to understand her.

Later, in the hospital, I asked her what she'd said. She was in an immense cast, traction like a cartoon strip. She had disappeared and become someone new. Her eyes were blackened, and she sucked water from an accordion-hinged straw. She said, "I guess I told you to get help." Her jaw was wired shut, but that wasn't why what she'd said hadn't sounded true. I felt that on the mountain she'd asked me something important, but also not obvious. Some secret available only to someone surprised and crushed after falling through the summer sky.

But besides the empty sound of her question, I recall nothing. In those moments on the hill there was shifting color; there was shape; but it tumbled without form or meaning, kaleidoscopic, as if I too were falling. The victims seemed dismantled by the plunge, not just injured but unformed. I ran again after Linda spoke to me, blindly following Kelly. Down, down, down. A flight over a quiet ski run, pursued by demons I would have years to get to know. Stopping to check my bleeding, I looked up at the bottom of another girl's shoes. We were spaced irregularly on the lift. Hers was probably the next occupied chair.

"What's going on?" she said. She was peevish. She swung her legs and chomped her gum. "Why aren't we going?"

It strikes me even now, as it did then, that what I was about to tell her would change her life. I felt the messenger's importance, a power I wouldn't feel again for many years until I was the one who had to tell my father his sister had died.

"They're hurt," I said. "It's bad."

She chewed her gum slowly, readjusted her headband, and tried to look back.

Then I heard a voice behind me say, "Lie down." I recognized a woman from the church camp. "Look, see," she said, "you're bleeding." She thought I was why Kelly had been so excited.

My glasses were sitting crookedly on my face. I feared they might cause her not to take me seriously, and I had something important to say. "It's not me who's hurt." Appearing worried then, she handed me a wrinkled tissue and trotted up the hill.

I realized my glasses' lenses were scratched. I'm extremely

nearsighted, and damaged glasses pose a frightening threat. "Kelly," I whispered below the ski lift, willing her return and my rescue, wishing I had gone with her, thinking how she'd escaped.

"Sh," the girl above me said. "I think I can hear them bawling."

I could hear the abrupt *tda-tda-tda* of winged grasshoppers and the purr of a few clover-seeking bees. The aspen trees seemed to tremble, and I wanted Kelly—and the old life she represented—more than I've ever wanted anyone in my life.

/ / /

Three years before, on the way to see the school nurse in fifth grade, Kelly had said, "I have a secret." Though Kelly called herself a tomboy, Kelly and her mother bought her dresses at J.C. Penney. They had attached petticoats that made a stiff elegant sound. While the rest of us wore saddle shoes, Kelly wore black patent-leather slip-ons, which she rubbed with Vaseline.

That day I suspected she loved Stephen Edison, and I presumed she was about to confess, maybe even tell me what it was like to be kissed. Instead she confided, "I have to wear deodorant."

"Deodorant?" This was excruciating, because I'd already started wearing deodorant and I hadn't thought to tell her first.

Kelly said, "You're so lucky not to have to." She combed her hair with her fingers and tossed it over her shoulders in the cold, world-weary way that girls with long hair learn. "What are you going to be when you grow up?"

"Teacher," I said, feeling doomed and lowly.

"I'm going to be a nurse in an operating room because my mom says I can think on my feet. Possibly I'll marry a doctor." Then, pitying me, she turned me toward her. "You'll be a great teacher because you remember all those things no one else cares about."

When I told my sister that Kelly was my best friend, she said, "Yeah, but are you hers?"

/ / /

My mother and our neighbor took me home from the hospital, where I hadn't needed treatment. My father had been called to the ski resort because he was the Mormon bishop. He found me on a stretcher in the back of the ambulance but stayed when it left because Sister Bennett, our camp leader, was being given blood and was not transportable. Everyone realized she was dying.

My mother had a car, but we rode home from the hospital in the neighbor's. I believe my mother accepted his offer because it seemed her part in what was expected: that she must be too distressed to trust herself to drive. Tragedy is about playing roles. I was already suffering the guilt of survival when she saw me in the emergency room and said, "Oh, Joan!" What was probably an expression of concern seemed to me an accusation.

The neighbor turned the car radio knob and the red needle glided through the numbers. He didn't say a word. Finally I asked, because no one volunteered it, "Who died?" My voice sounded strange and empty.

Maybe this is why my mother took the ride, so she wouldn't have to be alone with me and the question. She touched her throat. "Veronica," she said. "And Sister Bennett is very badly hurt."

The burden I'd assumed in asking was not what I'd expected, not the pain of loss but the difficulty of an appropriate response.

The fact was, I didn't feel like crying. I felt raw as my scraped face, but also stoppered. As my mother looked at me, most of all I wanted to be alone.

That night in my dreams white sheets hung from a clothesline. They floated, then dropped suddenly and became the humps of ghosts who chased me.

My mother's idea of comfort was to say, "Sh, sh, sh."

/ / /

The year I was born the top five names for girls were: K(C)atherine, Susan, Deborah, Karen, and Mary. Her name was Veronica Fuke. She never had a chance, you see. The first name was too exotic, the second blunt or angry or obscene. She licked her lips tentatively just before she spoke, and when she talked you noticed moist breathing. Asthma, I now guess. Her nose wasn't so much fat as flabby.

She was in 4-H. She grew vegetables with ignoble shapes or names: banana squash and rutabaga. Her family ate dehydrated fruit and were glad to show you their dehydrator—proud as though it were a new car. The boys at church teased her, which she took with such a diffuse lack of interest they were forced to stop. She had a blue mole by her eye; her little finger curved slightly inward.

I can't recall a single unkind, impatient, or angry thing she ever did. And I didn't like her. Worse, I didn't care about her. I don't know if I smiled at her, ever. There are bonds stronger than love. And what I know is that, if she'd lived, I'd have completely forgotten her. My behavior toward her then would not seem to matter now. So this is it: in her death I was caught, frozen in my indifference, an indifference nothing will ever help.

Her mother was pudding—soft with small, swollen feet. Later, she died of a tumor so big the whole congregation would watch it grow. It tugged at the shape of her formless dresses. She did not seek medical intervention and was patient in her suffering. Apparently the alternative—survival—seemed too perplexing or complicated to undertake. The elders gave her blessings and prayed for her return to health. But her daughter had been thrown from a ski lift. That might have proved something to her, or left her less susceptible to religion, more available to fate.

I want to believe Veronica died as calmly as her mother. If patience in death isn't courage, it's certainly the next best thing. I imagine Veronica surprised and then done with it, done with living on a day too beautiful to have given any warning. Perhaps she slipped out of life with simple grace.

The newspaper caption under her picture said, *Fell to her death.* I remember when I first read it, for some reason I thought it was *fell through* her death. And it seemed for a moment—though I knew better—as if she'd miraculously survived.

/ / /

The morning after the accident my mother made me go with her to see Veronica's mother. It didn't occur to me to protest.

"Sister Fuke," my mother said, "we want you to have this." She shoved something draped by a dishcloth. It takes on a bread shape as I see myself standing on that narrow porch, but it also reminds me of Veronica's own covered form beneath the ski lift. Veronica's mother wrapped her arms around it, hugged it. She had other children: a boy who later grew a straggly black beard to cover acne scars when he was only fifteen, a young daughter who would take to her stepmother with tenacious goodwill. But they were not around that day.

Veronica's mother bent toward me; her face was a haggard wilderness of suffering. I was young, still thought the worst pain was physical. Fascinated, I didn't know enough to look away. I wondered if this was what had turned Lot's wife into the pillar of salt.

Then I realized Veronica's mother was speaking to me. Too late, I saw her need. She said, "Honey, did Veronica say anything before she died?"

Grief, I saw, is shameless.

I looked to my mother, but she had slipped into her survival mode, become something firm and carefully closed. Behind Veronica's mother, I could see the clutter, newspapers scattered by the broken-down sofa. I knew where they kept some of their belongings: that there was a picture of Jesus ascending to glory in the living room, that a large yellow cat balanced on the edge of the kitchen sink and swatted at a spider plant. I saw how knowing those things hadn't stopped anything from happening, any more than the horseshoe that hung by the backdoor.

"Dear?" Veronica's mother whispered.

I knew I must lie. Such responses are instinctive, but I didn't know what to say.

"She just cried," I said. I spoke the lie humbly, knowing I'd failed her. Veronica's mother moved back into the room and suddenly she blurred, seemed to expand. It scared me until I realized that she'd moved into line with the scratched part of my lenses. She put the bread on the sofa and then slumped down herself.

When I called Kelly on the phone she said, "We must shut our eyes and promise to never even walk down their street again."

/ / /

My father spoke to the families with radiant conviction about life being eternal, which is, after all, a paltry comfort when there is still the whole of mortality to be somehow gotten through. At the funeral, he read Veronica's poem because her young cousin broke down, and he handed Sister Bennett's daughter his handkerchief. Then, right there, he raised money for a flagpole. Something had to be done, something to help us all sleep and eat and live. The flagpole was tangible, a solution. Its erection was an action, a counteraction to the falling. Something of an exchange.

It stood in front of the church with a stone wall behind it. *In memory of,* a plaque said. It gave the impression Sister Bennett had died for something, giving service to her camper girls. But of Veronica Fuke, what might be said? How do you make her noble? How do you make it feel as sad as it should when she wasn't particularly likable?

By Thanksgiving I was washing my hands between thirty and forty times a day. First my knuckles, then my fingertips became fiery and etched like Martian canals. They bled in the tender crusty valleys between my fingers. My mother took me to the doctor, who held them gently, as if touch could injure them more. "How are you sleeping?" he said, turning them over, and I knew he'd guessed.

Sometimes leaves blew off aspen trees in my dreams. Or newspapers fluttered from wire cages and then turned vicious as they flew toward me. *Sh, sh, sh,* I'd tell myself.

"Fine," I said. "I sleep OK." I knew better than to be found out.

On the remaining Fourth of Julys of my youth, we raised the flag at the church in a sunrise service. Then the deaths seemed patriotic.

/ / /

"Can you believe it?" the invitation crows, under a picture of a geriatric bulldog. "We've been out of high school twenty-five years!" I show it to Dave the way you show people your driver's license—hoping they won't laugh, but ready to join them when they do.

"You going?" he asks, pinching cilantro into Mexican salsa—his own recipe, of which he's overly proud. He's got a baseball cap on backward, which proves the seriousness of his chore.

"High school," I say, "is like a party where you drank too much. You hope you didn't embarrass yourself in ways you can't entirely recall."

"That, you see, just might be the fun of it—the amnesia factor, the wait and see." He plugs his mouth with a finger dipped in salsa.

"Needs more onion," I say of his recipe.

He wipes a hand on his apron. "You should go. They'll be glad to see you." He angles the knife in my direction in an unintentionally dangerous way. "Though they won't know you without your cat's-eye glasses." He growls and tries to nip at my ear.

I'm indignant. "In high school I wore contact lenses." We reserve our tenderest vanity for the least significant things.

/ / /

Two weeks later I'm waiting my turn in Optical Boutique. Suddenly this pops into my head: They bounced when they landed. No floating, none at all. Why is this revelation so amazing to me? Why does it seem so relevant?

The spectacles for sale are lined up in lighted glass cases. They look like Hollywood or synchronized swimming. I'll feel intrusive and clumsy when I take one from its place.

This: I have fallen from innocence. Fallen in love. On my face. Also into line. But this must be said: I *jumped* from the ski lift.

/ / /

Two other girls were hurt, injuries that changed their bodies as well as their minds, bones crushed in uncompromising ways. Linda would wear forever the appearance of an invalid—a shriveled arm, one leg shorter. But she also wore an expansive calmness, as if the accident had freed her of the worry of too much good fortune. I've heard she is an excellent mother, that she teaches business ethics and even plays the guitar.

The other girl, Kathy, became obese. She was addicted to pain medication, but also apparently to pain. She spoke about both with authority as well as awe, like a serious art collector. She'd been adopted as a baby, and in late adolescence went on a quest to find her birth father. When she found him in a big Eastern city, she slept with him, in what must have seemed a brilliant, definitive revenge.

It was called The Accident, as if there was or would only be one. There was occasional need for clarification about what exactly had happened, and so I was asked. It amazed me how I'd become an expert on this: the how of how people died.

/ / /

The summer before I started high school, I gave up washing my hands. I weaned myself slowly, using Jergens hand lotion as a crutch (its smell still makes me feel vulnerable). Then I painted my nails the color the seniors were wearing, a pearly white—

drama and sophistication both. My disgraceful hands became my glory. Isn't it so often so? I was known for having beautiful nails. Confidence is built on such small things.

Kelly and I went to the same high school, but she became dramatically out of date. Her rebellions were quaint and naive. She put cold cream and cornflakes on the math teacher's windows. She wrote toothless letters to the school newspaper's editor. Her popularity plummeted, and—I confess—I wasn't sorry. I had moved on. I had the stuff of high school success: nice legs, a smart mouth. Teenagers are merciless, a bit sadistic. What did I care that her petticoats no longer rustled? What did it matter when the world was exploding, blooming with forbidden pleasures—sinewy boys and smudgy-edged sins.

Kelly still had that sense of purpose. When the rest of us were painting on thick eyeliner and conscientiously cursing our parents, Kelly had school spirit and a quiet, too-tall boyfriend. You would see them on the school lawn, laughing or walking hand in hand into the dance. She had no need for subversion. She simply lacked outrage.

When my mother said, "I haven't seen Kelly in so long," I shrugged. "Yeah?"

My mother narrowed her eyes and said what she often did: "Is that any way to talk?"

"We don't have anything in common," I whined, because what can you have in common with someone after you've watched people die? We passed in school halls with only a "Hi there." Embarrassed like former lovers. Knowing we shared a guilty knowledge—the how of how people died. Or maybe she was shy because we were no longer friends. But our past connection was an impossible attachment, severed by an event of unbearable significance and terrible discovery. Mortality is not a subject a teenager should dwell on. And how can you be friends with someone who knows a secret as big as all that?

Only once do I remember us talking. I was at a church dance, sending a confused message to my nonmember boyfriend. She approached me while her boyfriend was outside to tell me her brother had received his mission call to Australia that her mother had been praying for. I thought how Kelly could do more with her appearance. For one thing, she should cut her hair. And I wondered how the accident had changed her. Had it taught her to be good or just to be unaware? Then suddenly I feared she'd talk about it, and I had no idea what I would say. But instead, she said, "You know, you have really pretty eyes," and I remember thinking how I wished she'd said that back when it would have counted, back when it would have done me some good.

In the yearbook under her picture, it said, "Girl most likely to stay out of jail."

/ / /

Years ago, at the end of trying to have a baby and getting to where it stopped hurting so much, Dave floated on our water bed and diagnosed me. "Obsessive-compulsive disorder," he said in an accent he claimed was Viennese.

"Getting up in the morning?"

"*Having* to get up in the morning. Stay," he said. "Let's eat brie and crackers and make crumbs and love. We'll send Queenie for the newspaper. We won't get up until we've renamed all the major cities in America."

The bed rocked as if it were keeping time. The clock radio was regrettably still. I said, "Is that any way to face life?"

"Aha!" he said, as if he'd caught me. "You don't *face* life. You *live* it." He was prone to mottoes of treacly optimism.

"I could stay in bed if I wanted." But I had to grip the blankets when I said it to keep from throwing them off.

"Couldn't," he said.

"Could." It seemed hard to breathe, though the blankets weren't at all close to my face. Concentrating, I counted but only got to five. "Long enough," I said. The cold air and being upright made it feel as if I'd won.

"Admit it," he yelled. He leapt to his feet on the bed, causing waves that he convincingly surfed in plaid boxers. "You *do* things. You fold every towel long, then short. You wipe off the table left to right. You floss!"

"To clean my teeth," I said, too primly, but then remembered suddenly the long-ago pleasure of washing my hands, knowing how important it was to keep moving. How could I explain it? The awful phrase: like a sitting duck.

/ / /

Sometimes I dream of snowfalls that are sucked back up into the sky. Once I dreamed of four waterbirds diving toward the earth, then suddenly swooping upward, sunlight glittering from the sequined eyeglasses they wore.

Sister Bennett had a nasally laugh I can no longer quite remember. She once told us, "For Pete's sake, drop the 'Sister Bennett.' You girls can call me Louise"—which we did, but only until she died. We loved her. Maybe that's why I don't speak of her. Maybe in loving her I've more successfully put her to rest.

Or perhaps she doesn't haunt me because she was not my age and even though she died, she couldn't have been me.

Veronica means "true likeness."

I wish I'd been friendly to Veronica Fuke.

I wish Kelly had come back for me, so that I wouldn't have had to go back up the hill and hear Sister Bennett moan or ride down the canyon alone in an ambulance.

Kelly sang "The Impossible Dream" in a chorus at graduation. Kelly didn't die.

/ / /

Quickly, before I can think what I'm doing, I get on a plane to go to my high school reunion. "Obsessive-compulsive disorder," I explain to Dave, who smiles in agreeable acceptance as he kisses me goodbye.

The reunion is at a water-slide park I didn't know existed, situated next to what we used to call the State Mental Hospital. Surely they've let all those folks go.

Can any place look as foreign as the place where you were born?

A man barks my name and embraces me. I have no idea who he is.

"Look at you," people keep demanding. "Will you just look at who's here?"

There's a man on the fringe of the group, left out of the hugs and squeals of enchantment, missing front teeth—old, surely not our age. Then someone places him. A boy who was left out back then or laughed at, still not included. But here he is, present, because it is *his* class, too.

Dependables of a high school reunion: only the people who were too skinny in high school are skinny at all. But also: the nice kids all became nice adults.

"Kelly's looking for you," my classmates tell me, as if we were best friends, as if I should even be here.

They show pictures of their children, who look more like themselves than they do. A classmate has died of an ominously initialed disease. "Didn't you know?" the others say to me. It occurs to me I did, but I've forgotten. Forgotten too how his widow married his best friend and for many that eased the pain.

Then Kelly's arms around me. She holds me like—of course, a long-lost friend—but also possessively. For a moment I think she holds me like her own child.

She whispers in my ear, "I'm sorry I made you jump."

"You didn't," I say.

"We *had* to jump," she says, looking for something in my face.

"Yes." It's an insignificant enough concession—and suddenly, possibly even true.

She has small blue eyes. When I notice the beak of her nose, I realize she resembles some kind of waterfowl. She is a handshaker, a woman who refers to herself by her last name. She doesn't put up with regrets or last chances or grudges. Before she tells me about how she became a school principal, or asks me how my father is, we have to talk about the accident. This is what reunion means, I think: the effort to make something whole.

She says they screamed as they fell.

"Yes," I say, "now I remember."

She says she lowered the footrest.

"You told me to roll when I landed," I say.

She shakes her head. "I must have gotten that from movies."

She tells me she spoke to each of them. Linda asked for help. Veronica didn't answer. And I feel a sick confirmation, all these years later, of how she'd already died. Kelly says she slept with her mother that night and dreamed she would raise a retarded child. She awoke knowing that would be her life. "It has been," she says simply, explaining her brain-damaged daughter.

I slap at a mosquito, wondering what causes what. Kelly tugs restlessly at her bangs, a mannerism so startlingly familiar I can't believe I'd forgotten it. She tells me her husband fell off scaffolding when they were dating, was impaled on rebar from two stories up.

"No—*fell?*" Are lives prone to motifs?

Her smile is rueful, as if the joke's on her. "But really, now he's fine."

When I don't say anything, she says, "Look. We jumped to save them." And I can see her going down the path below the ski lift, sure-footed, even wise. I think, though I do not tell her, that in jumping we saved ourselves. In the action, we exercised an option; we made an exclamation. We said, *We have survived.*

I can ask my classmates about Linda and Kathy, but I don't. It just feels like too much to know. Kelly sips the drink she's holding as she stands in front of the illuminated contortions of a water slide. I tell her about how lately I keep thinking about it.

She says, "That happens. What else would you expect?" Then, "You know, some good came of it." She means something spiritual. Mormons hope tragedy improves the soul. But for me, what I'd like is for the accident not just to have mattered but to surrender some kind of meaning. But it merely teases. The only thing that *feels* as if it's significant is that Sister Bennett was the same age we are now.

The park lights flicker.

I imagine the four of them, a grotesque sculpture garden in the moonlight, still lying beneath the ski lift, ten miles up the canyon at a ski resort a movie star now owns. They are stone blocks of ancient ruins, worn and weary of their work. And if we hadn't jumped? Would I then imagine us sitting there as well? Still? Action won't always save you, but it at least allows you to imagine you can be saved.

Here is the difference, I think suddenly: They fell to their deaths. We jumped to life. Instead of meaning, there is only that fact.

When the management locks us out of the water park, we stand under the unsteady lights of the parking lot and continue to tell our stories. "Fun as a blue M&M," I hear someone say. Kelly looks at me fondly. She bends to tie her Reeboks—now she's the one wearing sensible shoes. Then there are only a few of us remaining. Rhonda, still well-groomed and placid, talks about her book about monster trucks. Patty touches my arm, says, "You always had beautiful fingernails."

Suddenly it's just the two of us. Kelly puts her hands on my shoulders and turns me toward her. What I see in her face is not the child she was but, like a ghost, the grandmother she will shortly be.

I know what she'll say before she says it. "I'm sorry I didn't come back for you."

/ / /

My grandmother said, "Dreams are better than real, they're true." In mine, Dave and I go to a redwood forest. In a gift-shop cabin we buy a packet of seeds. On the back is this earnest plea: *The mighty sequoia is endangered. Please, kind traveler, germinate these seeds. Help us save our trees.*

I plant them in the backyard. First one, then thirty or forty. Oh, the pleasure of planting those trees! The delight of giving them names: Larkin (from the songbird), Ulysses (the cunning hero), Gabriel (with his Judgment Day horn). Names for the children we never had. But they grow like Jack's magic beans into shocking and unkempt adolescents. I tend them and try to talk them out of such unruly heights, but they slump and act disrespectful. They do forest wheelies, wear mirrored sunglasses, and smoke cigarettes.

I say, "I think I'll call California, see if they want them back."

Dave, of course, smiles and sings, "Let them be."

But in the backyard they're shoving each other. They've begun to leave messy fingerprints as they scrape the bottoms of clouds. Then suddenly I see a pattern. My trees are thick as a logjam, plugging up the summer air. You could step securely from one to another, like Towers of Babel. Everywhere you could walk up and down in the summer sky.

Mary Clyde was raised in Utah, has lived in New York City, and now resides in Phoenix, with her husband and five children. Her stories have been published in *American Short Fiction, Boulevard, Quarterly West,* and *Georgia Review.*

THE FLANNERY O'CONNOR AWARD FOR SHORT FICTION

David Walton, *Evening Out*

Leigh Allison Wilson, *From the Bottom Up*

Sandra Thompson, *Close-Ups*

Susan Neville, *The Invention of Flight*

Mary Hood, *How Far She Went*

François Camoin, *Why Men Are Afraid of Women*

Molly Giles, *Rough Translations*

Daniel Curley, *Living with Snakes*

Peter Meinke, *The Piano Tuner*

Tony Ardizzone, *The Evening News*

Salvatore La Puma, *The Boys of Bensonhurst*

Melissa Pritchard, *Spirit Seizures*

Philip F. Deaver, *Silent Retreats*

Gail Galloway Adams, *The Purchase of Order*

Carole L. Glickfeld, *Useful Gifts*

Antonya Nelson, *The Expendables*

Nancy Zafris, *The People I Know*

Debra Monroe, *The Source of Trouble*

Robert H. Abel, *Ghost Traps*

T. M. McNally, *Low Flying Aircraft*

Alfred DePew, *The Melancholy of Departure*

Dennis Hathaway, *The Consequences of Desire*

Rita Ciresi, *Mother Rocket*

Dianne Nelson, *A Brief History of Male Nudes in America*

Christopher McIlroy, *All My Relations*

Alyce Miller, *The Nature of Longing*

Carol Lee Lorenzo, *Nervous Dancer*

C. M. Mayo, *Sky Over El Nido*

Wendy Brenner, *Large Animals in Everyday Life*

Paul Rawlins, *No Lie Like Love*

Harvey Grossinger, *The Quarry*

Ha Jin, *Under the Red Flag*

Andy Plattner, *Winter Money*

Frank Soos, *Unified Field Theory*

Mary Clyde, *Survival Rates*